Little GIANTS

BY SHEILA BLACK

Willowisp Press

© 1994 Warner Bros.

Published by **Willowisp Press**;

a division of PAGES, Inc.

801 94th Avenue North, St. Petersburg, Florida 33702

Printed in the United States of America

2 4 6 8 10 9 7 5 3 1

ISBN 0-87406-749-9

PROLOGUE
1965

TWELVE YEAR OLD KEVIN O'SHEA strode confidently across the park, heading for the football field. His little brother, Danny, trailed after him, tossing a well-worn football into the air.

"Kevin O'Shea goes back to pass," Danny chirped, "sees his brother Danny down field. The ball is in the air. The O'Shea brothers are about to win the Super Bowl!"

The ball slipped out of Danny's hands. "Uh-oh," Danny shouted. "There's a fumble, and . . . ."

Danny looked up to see that his big brother was almost out of sight. "Hey, Kevin," he squeaked. "Wait up!" Danny scooped up the football and raced to catch up to his brother. "How many touchdowns you gonna score today? I'll bet at least fifty — maybe even a hundred!" Danny was so excited, he was practically bouncing up and down.

Kevin looked at him and sighed. "Danny?"

"Yeah?"

"What time did Mom say she was going to pick you up?"

A wide grin slid over Danny's face. "She's not. She said I could spend the whole day with you. Isn't that great?"

Kevin let out a long breath. "Yeah . . . great," he echoed in a flat voice.

Danny tossed the football high into the air again. He sprinted after it, just managing to catch it. "And the ball is intercepted by the great Danny O'Shea," he crowed.

"Hey, Danny," Kevin had drawn ahead again. "Hurry up! I've got to be on time. I'm captain of the team, remember?"

• • • • •

Kevin eyed Chris Hoyt, captain of the other team. "Spaces or laces?" he demanded seriously.

"Spaces," Hoyt replied.

Kevin gave the football a good spin. It whizzed around and finally tumbled over.

Kevin grinned. The laces were showing. "My pick," he said. "Now, let's see. I'll take . . . ."

A row of nine- to twelve-year-old boys gazed up at him, silently begging to be chosen. In the center of them stood Danny, grinning confidently; he was sure his big brother would pick him first.

"Butz," Kevin announced coolly.

Danny's face fell as Butz, a short stocky kid with a crew cut, eagerly ran up to stand behind Kevin.

"I'll take Stein," said Hoyt.

Danny looked up at Kevin, his eyes big and pleading like a puppy in a pet store window.

Kevin looked away. "Pinski," he said.

"McKormick," Hoyt made his pick quickly.

"Ralphy!"

"Mouse," Hoyt declared.

Danny glanced around. The only other kid who hadn't been picked was the new boy in the neighborhood — a big, clumsy-looking kid called Moretti. Kevin has to pick me now, Danny thought. He stared up at his brother. "Kevin," he whispered urgently. "Come on. Pick me! Please?"

Kevin hesitated. At last, he said in a loud voice, "Moretti." With a shy smile, Moretti trotted up to join the others.

"All right!" Kevin clapped his hands. "Let's get out there and play some football!"

"Yaaaahhh!" everyone shrieked. Danny watched numbly as the other kids happily hustled out onto the field.

"Hey Danny!" Kevin was calling him. Danny lifted his head hopefully. "The ball!" Kevin pointed at the football Danny was still holding. "Gimme."

Danny stared at his older brother. With every minute it was getting harder not to cry. "Man. I must be pretty bad if my own brother won't pick me," he mumbled.

"Danny . . . ." Kevin slowly walked over to him.

"Just go away." The hurt was evident in his voice. "I stink and you know it. You're perfect and I stink. End of story."

Kevin put his arm around Danny. "Come on, little bro'" he said. "It's just that I'm so great, it makes you look . . . really bad."

"Are you trying to cheer me up?" Danny demanded.

"Yeah."

Danny pulled away. "Well, it's not working."

Kevin grinned. "See? I stink at something, too." He grabbed the ball out of Danny's hand and ran smoothly back out onto the field.

"Aren't you playing, Danny?" said a girl's voice behind him.

Danny whirled around. It was Patty Murphy, the prettiest girl in the whole fourth grade.

"Hi Fatty . . . I mean Patty, " Danny stammered. "Naah, I'm . . . uh . . . on the injured list. Tore my leg muscle." Clutching his leg, Danny pretended to hobble off the field.

Patty watched Danny go, fingering the heart-shaped gold locket hanging from her neck. She smiled and shook her head as she saw Danny forget to limp.

Out on the field, Kevin was coming up for the punt when he looked over at Danny. He stopped and called, "Hey, Danny. Danny!"

"What?"

"You see that water tower?" Kevin pointed at the water tower that loomed over the park, with the words Urbania, Illinois painted on it. "One day our names are gonna be up there in big bold letters! The O'Shea Brothers! We're gonna own this town — you and me, buddy!" Kevin gave Danny the thumbs-up and turned back to the game.

Danny watched him, a slow smile lighting up his face.

"The O'Shea brothers," he murmured. "Yeah!"

Danny turned back toward the field as Kevin punted the ball. It was a perfect punt, Danny thought, just like everything Kevin did. But what about him? Danny gazed up at the water tower once more, his eyes shining with determination. Someday, somehow, he would do something great, too. But what?

CHAPTER ONE

Thirty Years Later

"C'MON, PEOPLE!" A GROWN-UP
Kevin O'Shea barked as he prowled up and down the sidelines.
"*Show* me something! Dig, dig, dig!" Kids of all shapes and sizes
hurtled themselves down the freshly-mowed football field. An
immense white water tower loomed above them. On it, in huge red
letters, were painted the words "Welcome to Urbania. Home of
Football's Kevin O'Shea!"

Kevin pushed his mirrored sunglasses higher on his nose. "I
said, DIG!" he hollered.

The kids pumped their legs faster.

Today was a big day in Urbania. Tryouts were being held for
Urbania's first-ever Peewee football team, and Kevin O'Shea, All-
American, and winner of the 1975 Heisman Trophy, was the
coach. The bleachers were crowded with parents, and the field was
jammed with football hopefuls. So far, though, they weren't
making Coach O'Shea very happy.

"Are you kidding me?" Kevin shrieked. "It's called SWEAT,
gentlemen. Now lemme see some!"

"Yeah," piped up a voice beside him. "Listen to Coach O'Shea.
Show some life out there." It was Butz. He was wearing a baseball
cap with the words "Assistant Coach" written across it.

Out on the field, the kids were going crazy. Everywhere you

looked, legs were pumping up and down, and the air was full of grunts and groans.

"All right," Kevin shouted. "Now, let's try a play!" Kevin called out instructions as the young players fanned out across the field. Butz punted the ball. A fat kid wearing an oversized blue sweatshirt caught it. Just as he was about to start running with it, however, a player wearing a green T-shirt charged into him. Pow! The fat kid was brought down with a sickening thud.

Watching from the sidelines, Butz grinned nastily. "Ouch!" he said. Kevin grinned, too. "Oooh baby, now that's what I call a play!" he said. Blowing the silver whistle around his neck, Kevin charged out onto the field.

The kid in the blue sweatshirt was lying belly up on the grass like a beached whale. The other kids were gathered around him. "Stand back," Kevin ordered, pushing his way through. "Give him some air."

Kevin turned to the player in the green T-shirt, who was leaning over the fat boy anxiously. "Nice pop, Icebox," he said grudgingly.

"Thanks, Uncle Kevin," said the kid in a high-pitched voice. Some of the kids on the field exchanged surprised glances. That kid sounded like a girl. Just then the player in green took off the helmet and shook out her long, brown hair. Her name was Becky O'Shea, and she was the daughter of Kevin's brother, Danny. "But I hope I didn't hurt him too much," she added.

Kevin glanced down at the kid in the blue sweatshirt. "Well, I think he'll live."

"You sure, Coach?" piped up Rasheed Hanon, a long-legged black kid, wearing a San Francisco 49er's helmet. "He looks dead."

"Yeah," added Tad Simpson, a skinny kid with red hair and freckles. "He ain't moving."

"You killed him, Icebox," said a blonde, freckle-faced boy named Patterson.

Becky kneeled down beside the fat kid. "Hey, Zolteck," she whispered. "Are you okay?" Zolteck let out a loud groan.

Becky reached down and pulled off Rudy Zolteck's helmet. Her eyes widened in horror as a thick reddish-brown substance oozed out from the helmet onto her fingers.

The other kids all gasped. "Ewww!"

"It's brain ooze!" someone shouted.

Kevin reached out to touch the gruesome stuff. His mouth fell open. "Peanut butter and jelly!?" He glared down at Zolteck, whose eyes were wide open now. "Are you insane?!"

Zolteck shrugged. Reaching into his helmet, he pulled out an extremely battered-looking sandwich and took a bite. "Still tastes good," he said.

Kevin grabbed the sandwich. "You'll never get anywhere using your helmet as a lunchbox, boy!"

"But I get hungry," Zolteck protested. The fat boy cautiously reached into his pocket and pulled out a crumpled-up bag. Butz snatched it.

"What is it now?" Kevin demanded.

"Cheetohs," came the reply.

Kevin shook his head in disgust. "Crunchy or puffed?"

Butz grinned. "Puffed."

"Wimp." Kevin turned back to Zolteck. "Now listen, kid. We're here to play football. Game-time, not snack-time. Think you can handle that?"

"Yes, sir, Coach O'Shea, sir," Zolteck mumbled.

"Good," Kevin said. "Let's get back to playing ball!" He motioned the kids to the other end of the field, where an obstacle course of tires had been set up. "Now I want to see speed and coordination. Becky," Kevin pointed at his niece, "you and Murphy take it first, okay?"

Becky nodded and trotted out to the obstacle course. Sean Murphy, a large, stocky kid, followed after her.

"One, two, three . . . go!"

Certain he could beat a girl, Murphy scrambled as fast as he could up the first obstacle — a mountain of stacked tires. But Becky matched him step for step. Murphy angrily sped up. Too fast!

He lost his footing and tumbled backwards, landing on his back with a loud crunch.

Kevin tooted his whistle. "Come on Murphy. Get up and do it." Murphy groaned and started up "Tire Mountain" again. Becky smiled back at him. Murphy glared at her. "I'll get you for this," he muttered.

• • • • •

Kevin stared down at his clipboard. The tryouts were half over, and he could see that putting together a winning football team wasn't going to be easy. Sure, there were a few kids who could play, but the rest of them were hopeless.

"Okay, line up," Kevin shouted, waving the kids over to the end zone. "Let's see if any of you can run. Briggs, you first."

A tall, confident-looking boy ambled out on to the field. Kevin took a stopwatch from his pocket. "Go!" he shouted.

Briggs sprinted rapidly to the forty-yard line.

"8.5 seconds. Excellent, Briggs. Next."

All eyes turned to Tad Simpson. The scrawny, red-haired boy reluctantly stumbled to the starting line. "Okay, ready," he squeaked.

Kevin pressed down to start the stopwatch. "Go!"

Arms flailing and legs wobbling, Tad zigzagged slowly out to mid-field. With every step, he looked closer to tripping over his own feet. Kevin shook his head. This kid was a total spaz. "What is this, a telethon?" he demanded. "Next!"

Some of the boys watching cracked up, but Becky called out, "It's okay Tad. Way to go." Tad lifted his head and smiled.

Murphy, who was next to Becky in line, sneered. "Hey, Tad! Way to go," he mimicked her.

"Shut up, Murphy."

"Hey, Icebox," Murphy leered at her, "you look like a boy, you play like a boy. So . . . can you prove you're not a boy?"

Patterson snickered. "Yeah. Go on and prove it, Icebox. Bet you can't, though, 'cause you're not a boy, and you're not a girl. You're a freak!"

Quick as lightning, Becky jumped Patterson and paralyzed him in a vicious headlock.

"Owwww!" Patterson gasped. "Stop! I can't breathe!"

Becky grinned. "Yeah, well, that's kinda the whole point."

"Becky! Let him go!"

Becky looked up. Her dad was standing on the sidelines. He had just come from work and was still wearing his greasy mechanic's overalls.

"Hi, Daddy." Becky tightened her grip on Patterson.

"I mean it, honey. *Right now!*"

Becky slowly lifted her arm from around Patterson's neck. Patterson stumbled to his knees, his face as red as a ripe tomato. Becky looked at him. "You're lucky my dad showed up, pal . . . " she threatened.

Becky turned back to her father. "How long have you been here?"

"Just got here. Good luck, Beck. I'll be watching from the stands, okay?" Danny waved and walked over to where Kevin's wife, Karen, and seven-year-old daughter, Priscilla, were sitting.

"How's Becky doing?" he asked as he sat down.

"She's the best one out there, Uncle Dan," Priscilla replied.

•　•　•　•　•

"Next is passing and catching." Kevin sent the football spiraling through the air. "I don't have to tell you why passing and catching are important, do I? Good. Now, let's see how your hands are." He pointed at the black kid in the 49er's helmet. "Hanon, get out there."

"Yes, Coach." Hanon jogged out to mid-field. Butz lobbed him a high, fast pass. Hanon jumped for it and missed. Butz threw a slow pass. Hanon missed that one, too, and the next three passes Butz sent him.

Kevin rolled his eyes. "The kid's fast, but —"

"Fifth one he's booted." Butz finished the thought for him.

"Yeah," Kevin sighed. "Hands like frying pans." He raised his voice. "That's enough, Hanon. Next!"

Hanon jogged slowly to the end of the line. He held out his hands and stared down at them sadly. "Why are you doing this to me, fellas?" he asked plaintively. "Come on. Don't I treat you good? I cut your nails, I wash you, and —"

"Hey, Hanon," Murphy nudged him in the ribs. "You ever catch *anything? Ever?*"

Hanon frowned. "Yeah. Caught a cold yesterday, Murph. Here. Have some!" He sneezed messily all over Murphy.

"Hey! Gross! Get offa me!'

The other kids burst out laughing.

Just then Kevin's whistle sounded.

"Tryouts are over," Kevin shouted. "Everybody over here. Come on. Line up!"

The kids raced to the right sideline, where a podium had been set up at the fifty-yard line. This was the moment they had been waiting for. They watched eagerly as Kevin climbed up to the podium and leaned into the microphone.

"Can everybody hear me?" Kevin asked.

"Yes!" came the shouts of reply from the kids on the field and their parents in the bleachers. "Good," Kevin said and launched into his speech.

"You know," he began, gazing earnestly out into the crowd. "I'm reminded of what a lucky guy I am. Lucky to be born an O'Shea . . . " Becky looked over at Danny and mouthed Kevin's next words before he spoke them. " . . . .Lucky to be born in this great town, and lucky to be blessed with the abilities that allowed me to bring something back here to Urbania." Becky and Danny grinned. They had both heard Kevin give speech like this before. Kevin went on. "Little things like three high school championships, a National Collegiate Championship, an All-American title, not to mention a Heisman Trophy."

The crowd erupted into cheers.

"And today," Kevin went on, when everyone had finally quieted down. "I'm even luckier, because there's one more thing I can bring to this town: A *Peewee Football League State Championship!*"

"Hooray!" the kids and their parents cheered wildly. "Let's hear it for the colossal Kevin O'Shea! Let's hear it for the new coach!"

Kevin flashed a victory sign, then motioned for silence.

"Okay, kids," Kevin grinned. "When you hear your name called, come on up and get your jersey."

Across the stadium kids and their parents held their breath. All eyes turned to Butz, who was carefully lifting a stack of brand new blue football jerseys out of a large cardboard box. Although the kids were tired, sweaty, and covered in dirt, their eyes were bright with anticipation.

"Oh man," Becky stood up on her tiptoes, "those jerseys are so cool!"

"Yeah." Zolteck poured a stream of Reese's pieces down his throat. "I get dibs on Joe Montana's Number 15 —"

"And I'm getting Michael Irvin's number," said Hanon solemnly. "The big 88."

Up on the podium, Kevin turned the pages of his clipboard, calling off names. "Briggs . . . Patterson . . . Hoffs . . . Lewis . . . Bookman . . . Grabelski . . . Rivers . . . Scanlon . . . ."

The entire football stadium shook with cheers. The kids who had been chosen and their parents whooped and hollered. But the kids who hadn't been chosen stared up at Kevin, clenching their fists and waiting.

Becky glanced over at her father. He smiled encouragingly.

Kevin was still flipping through the pages on his clipboard. "Parkhurst . . . Walker . . . Beaurigard . . . Gibbs . . . Greeson . . . Curry . . . ." Kevin paused. "And last but not least," he added dramatically, "the backbone of our team . . . ."

Becky glanced over at her Dad with a proud smile.

"Sean Murphy!"

Murphy let out a whoop. Pushing Becky aside, he tore up to the podium, his arms raised over his head like Rocky Balboa.

Becky rocked back on her heels, stunned. She watched as Murphy and the other members of the new team traded high-fives. She had never felt so miserable in her whole life.

The other kids who hadn't been picked felt the same way. Tad

Simpson's jaw wobbled and tears spurted out of his eyes. Hanon buried his head in his dad's old football jacket. As for Zolteck, he let his bag of Reese's pieces slip out of his hand, sending the bright-colored candies scattering all over the ground.

"I don't believe it," he said morosely. "I know I'm not the greatest player in the world, but —" he turned to Becky "— not picking you, Icebox? That's crazy. You're the best there is!"

"I guess Uncle Kevin doesn't think so," Becky mumbled. She lowered her head and bit her lip. She didn't want anyone — especially her Dad — to see that she was crying.

● ● ● ● ●

Danny stared over at Becky and the other kids who hadn't been picked. He knew just how they felt. *Awful.* He looked up at Kevin, who was talking to the Mayor. How could his brother do this?

Danny fought his way through the crowd over to Becky and her friends. He kneeled down in front of Tad Simpson who was bawling his eyes out.

"I'm sorry," Danny said earnestly. "This totally bites, but . . . maybe you can learn something from this . . . ."

"Yeah," Tad sniffled, "not to try out for anything."

"Not in a hundred years," agreed Zolteck.

"Not in a hundred million years," put in Hanon.

"Not ever," declared Becky fiercely.

Danny looked at them. Suddenly, his jaw tightened. "Wait right here," he told Becky. He turned and marched directly to his brother.

● ● ● ● ●

"So Coach?" Mayor Kelly asked. "What do you think?"

"I like what I saw, Mayor," Kevin replied.

Mayor Kelly smiled. "Me, too, Kev. Fact is, I made a little bet with the Mayor of Sutterville, and now . . . . Well, I guess he's gonna be buying me a steak dinner. Hey there, Danny!"

Danny barely answered. "Hey." He turned to Kevin. "What the heck are you doing?"

Kevin sighed. "Putting together a championship football team, little bro'.""Yeah? Well what about those other kids? Did you see their faces —"

"Danny," Kevin interrupted him, "football is not about faces. It's about speed. Talent. I picked the best players."

Danny took a deep breath. "Hey . . . look, little bro'," Kevin smiled, "I've only got three weeks to get ready. I can't be wasting my time with a bunch of —"

"Losers," Butz broke in.

"Butz!" Kevin said warningly.

"I mean who do you think you are?" Danny went on. "Vince Lombardi? This is Peewee football, Kevin. Everybody should get a chance to play."

"Not on our team!" Butz declared.

"Put a zipper on it, Butz!" Danny turned back to Kevin. "What about Becky? She's better than any of those boys."

Kevin threw up his hands. "I hate to break it to you, Danny, but Icebox is a *girl*. Maybe if you start *treating* her like one, she'll finally start *acting* like one."

"I don't need you to tell me how to raise my daughter!"

"And I don't need you to tell me how to put together a football team."

Kevin strode over to his brand-new Corvette and slid into the front seat. After a moment, Danny marched over and leaned his head in the window. "What about those kids, Kevin? You hurt their feelings, Kevin," he burst out.

Kevin rolled his eyes. "Danny. Listen. You and I both know . . . those kids just don't cut it. What am I supposed to do — lie to 'em? Build their hopes up? They'll thank me tomorrow."

Danny let out a long, slow sigh. How many times had he heard Kevin say that when they were growing up. A thousand times? Ten thousand times? "You really think so?" he muttered.

Kevin hadn't heard him. "I knew you'd see it my way, " he said with a grin as he backed up and drove away.

CHAPTER TWO

BECKY WATCHED HER DAD JUGGLE
two cans of ravioli. It was 7:00 p.m. She and Danny were in the
kitchen, throwing dinner together. "Hey, watch it!" she said, as one
of the cans crashed to the floor. "You almost broke my foot!"
Danny shrugged, picked up the can, and started juggling again.
This time it went better. "Woo!" said Becky. "What a pro."

"Yeah." Danny replied with a grin. He opened the cans of
ravioli, dumped them into a dish, and stuck it in the microwave.

Becky rinsed off some lettuce. She wrapped a dishtowel around
it and shook it vigorously to dry it. "You know, Dad," she said after
a moment, "my friends and I would be great to have on a team. I
know it!"

Danny looked at her. "Of course you would," he said.

Becky frowned, put the lettuce in a bowl and poured some
bottled thousand island dressing on it. A few moments later the
ravioli was ready. "Dinner-time!" Danny sang out, taking two
plates from the cupboard.

Becky was still frowning. "It isn't fair," she said. She sat down
at the table. "I'm as good as any of one of those jerks, and my
friends could get better."

Danny sat down across from her. "You're right," he said. "I
can't believe Kevin is still getting away with this kinda . . . ."

"Crap!" Becky finished for him.

"Exactly! Watch your language."

Becky made a goofy "Come on, Dad," face, then her
expression became serious again. "I hate not being picked."

"I know, sweetheart." Danny smiled at her. "But, listen, I have
an idea. Let's put some big mud tires on the go-cart."

Becky hesitated. Normally, she loved working on her go-cart. Her father had made it for her last birthday, and it was the coolest go-cart in the world. It was silver and black with "Icebox" painted on the side. Becky drove it everywhere, and she knew mud tires would come in handy, but . . . . Becky shook her head. "Nah. I don't wanna."

"Okay, forget the tires. Let's go camping and make moose sounds in the woods."

Becky scowled and shook her head again. "Nah."

"Yeah. I hate moose sounds, too . . . . So . . . I know. Instead, let's invent a magic potion that makes you sixty-three feet tall and sing like Alvin and the chipmunks."

"Dad!" Becky smiled in spite of herself. "You don't have to do this, you know."

Danny put his arm around her shoulders. "Yes, I do. You might not believe this, but I know exactly how bad you feel — not getting picked. But maybe you're just not looking at it right," he went on.

"What do you mean?"

"Well, Beck . . . . You know when Mom told us she was going to have to do what was best for her?"

Becky bit her lip and nodded.

"Well, when she chose to leave, she was making a choice for us, too. She kind of gave us the chance to get real close, right?"

Becky hesitated, then slowly nodded again.

"So, when Uncle Kevin didn't pick you for the team, maybe it was the same kind of thing," Danny said. "'Cause now you're free to be picked for something else. Hey, who knows, you may even turn around and do a little picking of your own."

"Dad." Becky's tone made it clear she didn't buy what he was saying for a second. "I just want to play football."

"I know, sweetie," Danny said. "And believe me, if I had a football team, I'd pick you."

Becky sighed. "I know you would, Dad," she said. "But you don't have a team and Uncle Kevin does." Then the two of them finished the rest of the meal in silence.

• • • • •

It was Sunday, the day after the Peewee League tryouts, and the sun was once again shining brightly. Just about everyone in Urbania was in a good mood — everyone that is, except for a group of kids who sat splayed out in front of an old wooden go-cart shed near Danny's gas station.

The shed was clearly some kind of clubhouse, with hand-lettered signs nailed all over it. The overgrown lawn out front was littered with rusty lawn chairs, torn up armchairs, a saggy, old couch and a number of strange looking contraptions — a couple of which were actually go-carts.

Zolteck leaned back in his armchair and stared up at the sign he had just hung over the front door. It said "Losers' Club" in big, black letters.

"Yeah. Losers' Club," Zolteck grunted, punching the football in his lap. The ball was a weird orange color because, like everything else Zolteck touched, it was covered with Cheetoh crumbs. "That's us all right. Big fat losers!"

Nubie, a skinny kid with wild, curly hair and mad-scientist glasses, raised his eyebrows. "Don't you think you guys are taking this a little too much to heart?" he asked, looking around at the glum faces around him. "I mean, it's just a game."

"Just a game?" Hanon stared at him in disbelief. "Nubie, man, this ain't just a game. It's football!"

"And we don't get to play it," said Tad Simpson gloomily.

"You said it." Zolteck punched his Cheetoh-covered football again. "You're all welcome to try out again next year," he mimicked Kevin's voice. "Life sucks."

"Yeah." Hanon shook his head sadly. "There goes my shot at the pros. Now I guess I'm just going to have to be a senator or something."

"My mom says I've got to take piano lessons now," sighed Tad. "The teacher is 86 years old, and he smells like pepperoni and Vicks vapor rub. I'm DEAD."

Nubie raised his eyebrows. "Pardon my ignorance, but why are you guys so obsessed with playing football?"

Hanon looked at him. "We're kids!"

"Ah." Nubie snapped his fingers. "Of course."

"Man," said Tad after a moment. "I really hate those guys."

"Yeah, me, too!" agreed Zolteck. Sticking his hand under his armpit he made a loud farting noise, then another, and another. "Here's a kiss for Murphy. And one for Patterson and Briggs, too," he giggled.

"Don't forget one for the great Coach O'Shea," put in Hanon.

"Don't worry. I won't," replied Zolteck, letting another one fly.

"Ugh!" the others cracked up and pretended to hold their noses. Suddenly, a voice behind them said. "Gross, Zolteck! What kind of road kill did your mom feed you last night?"

The kids whirled around. It was Murphy. He, Patterson, and Briggs had snuck up on them! The kids could see their bikes parked over by the side of the shed.

Zolteck glared at them. "Free range skunk. Now, scram!"

"What did you say?" Murphy took a step closer.

Nubie stood up. "Excuse me, gentlemen," he said politely, but firmly. "This is a private establishment."

"Yeah," said Tad. "Get out of here!" He paled as Murphy turned toward him. "P-p-lease?"

Murphy eyed him. "I'm hurt, okay?" the big kid said.

"Yeah," put in his friend, Briggs. "I mean we just came by to tell you guys how incredibly sorry we are that you didn't make the team . . . ."

The members of the newly-formed Losers' Club exchanged astonished glances, but just then Murphy, Patterson, and Briggs burst out laughing. "NOT!" they shrieked. Lunging forward, they grabbed Nubie by the ankles and hoisted him into the air.

"Please don't," Nubie asked politely.

Ignoring him, the three bullies raised him higher and tugged his legs apart.

"Yeeeeoooowwwww!" Nubie shrieked.

"Drop him!" Murphy commanded.

They tossed Nubie into the air, and he landed with a yelp.

"Ooooh, did that hurt?" Murphy asked. Then he turned to Tad. "Hey Tad-pole, how 'bout I give you a chance to prove you're a real man by calling you out?"

"C-c-calling me out?" Tad stammered.

"Yeah, for a one-on-one fight with me." Murphy grinned.

Tad turned green. "How 'bout I give you a chance to prove you're a saint instead, by begging for your absolute, unconditional mercy?"

Murphy snorted. "Give me a break, Tad-pole."

At that moment, they heard the whine of an engine. It grew louder and louder. Murphy, Patterson, and Briggs looked at each other. "Uh-oh," all three shouted at once. "The Icebox!"

Now everyone could see Becky roaring toward them in her silver-and-black go-cart. She was wearing her skull-and-crossbones helmet and her favorite song, Jimi Hendrix's "Foxy Lady," was blaring on the go-cart's tape machine.

"Oh, no!" Murphy, Briggs, and Patterson let go of Tad and went racing for their bikes. Meanwhile, Tad and the others burst into cheers. "Go! Get 'em, Icebox!" they shouted.

Murphy, Briggs, and Patterson were peddling away as fast as they could. Becky grinned and started after them.

The three bullies tore across the road and down into the ravine on the other side that led to a path that ran along Urbania's largest creek. Becky followed.

After a moment, the Losers' Club took off after her, stopping at the bridge suspended above the ravine. Zolteck pulled out a pair of binoculars and gazed through them. "What's going on?" Hanon demanded.

Zolteck chuckled. "She's following Patterson." Just then the kids heard a scream, followed by a loud splash.

They looked up at Zolteck. He made a thumbs-up sign.

"Patterson is in the creek," he declared solemnly.

"All right!" said Hanon. "One down, two to go."

"Who's she chasing now?" Nubie wanted to know.

Zolteck squinted into the binoculars. "Briggs!" he replied.

"He's trying to pull some fancy stuff. Side-to-side moto-crosses. Wheelies over tree stumps. But the Icebox is staying on his tail."

Zolteck frowned. "Uh-oh. Briggs is pulling away. Looks like he might escape. Wait! The Icebox is turning up the heat. She's pulling even with him. He just bumped into her antenna. He's fighting to hang on, but . . . ."

There was another scream and another loud splash.

"In the creek?" asked Tad eagerly.

Zolteck grinned and nodded. "Chalk up number two."

"What about Murphy?" said Hanon.

Zolteck lifted his binoculars again and shook his head. "Murphy's made it," he said flatly. "He's heading down the road back to town."

"Oh, yeah?" said Tad. "Let's go after him!"

The kids ran for their bikes and started down the road. Becky was just ahead of them. Suddenly, Becky pulled off to the side of the road.

"What's she doing?" yelped Hanon, hitting his breaks.

"Stopping," said Nubie, skittering to a halt just behind him. "In fact, I believe this is Sean Murphy's residence."

"Ohhhh!" said the others. They cautiously got off their bikes. Becky was still sitting in the go-cart, the engine idling.

Just then, they spotted Sean Murphy. He was standing in the driveway, beside his bike. Unfortunately he wasn't alone. Five of his Cowboy teammates were with him, and they all looked red-hot, hopping mad.

"Uh-oh," said Tad, turning a horrible shade of green.

"You said it," muttered Zolteck.

Murphy took a step toward them, his friends close behind him. "Would I give anything to get you guys back out on the field this minute," he said.

Becky revved her engine. "That's enough, Murphy!"

Murphy stopped in his tracks. So did his friends.

"Anyhow, don't worry. You're gonna get your chance."

Murphy looked at her. "What did you say, Icebox?"

"You heard me."

Murphy shook his head. "Uh, either I'm a total retard or you're forgetting that you and the spaz patrol here didn't make the team."

Becky jutted out her chin. "Yeah? Well, Murph, we've got a little news flash for you. *We've got our own team!*"

Hanon's eyes popped open. "We do?"

"Yeah," echoed Zolteck. "We do?"

"What team?" asked Tad, turning even greener.

"Our team." Becky replied. She nodded at Murphy. "Yeah, you heard right. *We've got our own team.* So call your oh-so-cool coach and break the bad news. 'Cause we're gonna whomp, we're gonna stomp, and we're gonna kick butt all over Urbania!!!"

Murphy and the other Cowboys' mouths fell open.

"You've got to be joking," Murphy said. "If you guys have a team, who's your coach?"

Becky hesitated a moment. "My dad."

"Your dad?" Tad looked like he was about to faint. "We're gonna die!"

Murphy and his friends burst out laughing.

Becky shot Tad a look. "Thanks a lot," she mouthed at him.

"I'm sorry!" Tad whispered back. "But . . . we are!"

"No, we're not!" Becky pressed her foot down on the accelerator and spun out a 360, kicking up great gobs of mud onto Murphy and the other Cowboys.

Murphy's face turned brick red. "That's it, Icebox!" he shouted. "I'm going to get you for this!"

"Go ahead and try," Becky shot back, speeding away.

"Our own team?" said Hanon wonderingly.

"Might not be bad," said Zolteck.

"Uh, guys, I think we better . . . ." Tad gestured at Murphy and his friends, who were charging towards them.

"Yes, gentlemen," said Nubie, leaping on to his bike. "I strongly suggest we get out of here — while we still can!"

They frantically pedaled down the road.

CHAPTER THREE

BAM! KEVIN O'SHEA REACHED UP and easily caught the football that Butz lobbed at him from across the Chevrolet showroom floor. Pulling a pen from his pocket, he signed the ball with a flourish.

"Here you go, Mr. Green," he said. "There are only a few times in a man's life when he can howl at the moon: when he gets married, when he has a baby, when he scores a winning touchdown, and when he buys his very first Chevy. Congratulations!"

"Gee, thanks, Mr. O'Shea." Mr. Green climbed into his new car and drove it off the lot.

Kevin turned to Butz. "What can I tell you, Butz? I'm a winner." He glanced up at the Heisman Trophy prominently displayed in a glass case against the wall. "I'm going to lunch. Put my Heisman back in the safe, and," Kevin paused for a moment, "if you wanna surprise me, sell a car today."

Kevin hopped into his Corvette and went zooming down Main Street. As he drove along, everyone stared. Mothers pushing their babies in strollers waved at him. Old codgers took off their hats to him. A paper boy shouted, "Have a paper, Mr. O'Shea, sir!" and tossed the paper through the open window of the car. Even the cop at the main intersection of town gave Kevin a thumbs-up.

Kevin pressed his foot on the accelerator, running a red light. The cop stared after him. "I wish he wouldn't do that," he said. But Kevin was long gone. In fact, he was pulling into the parking lot of the Coffee Cup Cafe, Urbania's most popular diner.

"Hey, it's Kevin O'Shea," cried Wilbur, one of the regulars, from the booth in the back as Kevin entered the diner.

"Sure is!" said his brother, Orville. "Come sit down and tell us again all about how you won the Orange Bowl."

"Sure thing, gentlemen." In no time at all, a crowd had gathered, and Kevin was leading them on a journey down Memory Lane — a play-by-play review of all the great moments in the phenomenal career of the colossal Kevin O'Shea, Urbania's own football hero.

" . . . See, we're down by six," Kevin was saying, "and it's third and goal with two seconds left. I've been hit so many times I can't even *see* straight —"

"Two seconds!" Wilbur interrupted.

"Could have swore it was three," said Orville.

"I thought it was four, " said Wilbur

Kevin groaned. "Guys, believe me, it was two! Look, here's how it went, fellas. All eyes were on me. It was so quiet you could hear a pigeon sigh, and I'm wondering what to do, when suddenly I hear a sweet, solemn, soulful voice from the heavens say —"

"O'Shea, you moron! You'd better have a darn good explanation for this. That's all I can say!" broke in a voice.

Kevin looked up, startled. "Mayor Kelly!"

"That's right!" The Mayor frowned at him. "And we've got to have a talk, right now."

Kevin smiled at the guys around the table. "'Scuze me, gents. Peewee business. What's up, Kelly?"

"You've made me look awful foolish, son."

"What in heck are you talking about?" Kevin demanded.

"The tempest in our Peewee teapot," the Mayor replied dramatically. "Now, I got Urbania in this Pop Warner Peewee League 'cause I told everybody that the colossal Kevin O'Shea was going to lead our boys. Then today I get this call. Seems there are two teams in this town! What in tarnation is going on?"

"*Two* teams? Who's coaching the other one?"

"An O'Shea, that's who," the mayor growled. "Your baby brother, Danny!"

• • • • •

Danny strolled into the Coffee Cup Cafe and sat down at the counter. The waitress, Agnes, slid him a menu. "Hey, Danny. What'll it be today?"

"Nothing 'O'Shea,'" Danny muttered gloomily. "What's the special, Agnes?"

"Chicken," Agnes paused. "O'Shake and Bake."

Danny frowned and shook his head.

"How about some catfish, then?"

Danny brightened. "That sounds good."

"One O'Shea Fillet Flambe?"

Danny put his head in his hands. "There is no escape," he groaned. "Just a coffee, Agnes. Thanks."

He lifted his head to see Becky standing beside him. "Dad!"

"Yes?"

"I got something to tell you . . . ." Becky glanced nervously toward the corner of the diner. Danny now noticed that Kevin was there, talking to Mayor Kelly.

"Sure, Becky. What is it?"

"I took your advice," Becky said quickly. "Me and the guys, we're forming our own football team." She leaned down and kissed him on the cheek. "Love you a lot. See you!"

She turned and ran out. Danny gazed after her in bewilderment. "Becky, wait! That's great . . . "

Danny broke off as his extra-large brother leaned over him. Kevin's jaw was set, and his eyes were spitting fire.

"Kevin. Hey. What's up?"

"Are you trying to make me look like an IDIOT? What's all this junk about you coaching another team?" Kevin snapped.

"Me coaching another team?" Danny echoed in astonishment. He glanced over to the door of the cafe. Becky was standing just outside it. She stared back at him, with her hands together as if she was praying.

"Please," she mouthed. Zolteck and Hanon were beside her. They, too, gave Danny a pleading look.

Danny turned back to Kevin. "Kevin, I'm not coaching. I just heard about this . . . ..

"You'd better *believe* you're not coaching," Kevin exploded. "You can't coach football! You've never even played football —"

"And who's fault was that?" Danny broke in.

"Don't change the subject!" Kevin roared. "The point is, those kids could get seriously *hammered* out there. I mean, when I heard you had a team, I almost had a heart attack."

"Hey! I'm not coaching, okay? Enough already."

"You bet you're not coaching," Kevin was on too much of a roll to stop now. "I mean, nobody ever said life was fair, right? The way I see it? Some of us run touchdowns . . . and some of us run the class projector."

Danny was starting to lose his temper. "What's wrong with running the class projector? I RAN THE CLASS PROJECTOR!"

"Yeah, and I'm sure you were a great projectionist —"

"Can it, Kevin, okay?"

"Look Danny," Kevin sighed, "the point is, you wanna work with those kids? Form a club or something? Fine. But keep out of the big-boy stuff, okay?"

Danny glared at him.

Kevin decided to try another approach. "Listen, Danny, I know how you feel. It's not the kids' fault they're no good. A lot of terrible football players end up running the *country*, right? Some of them even win Nobel *Prizes*. Could Einstein score a touchdown? No way! Did anybody care? Not on your life!"

The entire cafe was all ears now. Everyone in Urbania had seen Kevin and Danny O'Shea argue before, but never like this.

"Let me see if I understand, Kevin," Danny said in a dangerously quiet voice. "You're all for me doing something with these kids as long as it's not football, right?"

Kevin's face relaxed into a smile. "You've got it, little bro'. Keep out of football and everything'll be hunky-dory."

Danny didn't say anything.

"I knew you'd see it my way," Kevin clapped him on the back. "Don't worry, Danny. You'll thank me tomorrow."

Danny froze. "You'll thank me tomorrow?" he echoed. He gritted his teeth and looked up. Kevin was already walking away.

"No," Danny said quietly, then more loudly, "No, I won't!"

Kevin turned around in surprise. "Excuse me?"

"You heard me," Danny retorted. "And I'll tell you something else. I *don't* see it your way. I've *never* seen it your way." His voice rose. "I HATE YOUR WAY!"

Kevin looked stunned. "Danny! What's gotten into you?"

"*You!* You've gotten into me! And I'm sick of it. We're forming our own team!"

"What are you — nuts?" Kevin shouted. "League rules clearly state one town, one team. You *can't* have two teams.

"Let's have a playoff," Wilbur shouted from the corner. "The winner gets to be the town's team!"

"Great idea, Wilbur," Orville chimed in. "How about it fellas? A playoff!"

Danny hesitated. How could his team possibly play Kevin's? He had never coached anything, let alone football. "I . . . ." Danny glanced around helplessly. Then he saw Becky and her pals standing over by the door. They were looking at him, their eyes still wide and pleading. Sure, they looked scared, but they looked determined, too. They *wanted* to play, and they *wanted* him to coach them.

"How about it, Kevin? Two Saturdays from today. At twelve noon. We'll meet you at half court —"

Becky's shouted through the door, "Dad, that's the fifty-yard line."

Danny shrugged. "Whatever."

Kevin sagged like a punctured balloon as Becky and the other kids started cheering. Orville and Wilbur were smiling and nodding. "Good for you, Danny," Orville called out. "Nice to see you show some spunk."

Becky grinned proudly. "Way to go, Dad!"

Kevin shook his head. "You don't stand a *chance*, little bro'."

"We just want to play," Danny replied as he headed out the door toward Becky and her friends.

CHAPTER FOUR

DANNY PEERED INSIDE THE GO-CART
shed. In the dim light from the single overhead bulb, he could just make out Nubie's frizzy hair and wire-rimmed glasses. Nubie was hunched over a chess board, playing a game of speed chess against himself.

"Hey," Danny said.

Nubie looked up and shook his head. "Sorry, Mr. O'Shea," he said firmly, banging the clock for his next move. "If you've come about your football team, forget it!"

"Don't you want to at least hear what I have to say first?"

"Nope." Nubie moved his black queen, putting the white king in check. "See, Mr. O"Shea, I have an aversion to pain and suffering. There are 207 bones in the human body, all of them highly breakable. That's why I tend to stay away from high-risk areas such as playgrounds, 7-11 parking lots, and most important, any and all football fields!"

"Look, Nubie," Danny said quickly. "I don't actually want you to be on the team, all right? In fact, you don't even have to set foot on the field. What I want you to do is be my assistant coach. See, I need an assistant who will help me create plays."

Behind his coke-bottle-thick glasses, Nubie's eyes gleamed. "What kind of plays?" he demanded.

Danny smiled. "Creative plays. The kind you're used to creating on a chess board, but —"

"Wow!" Nubie was starting to get excited. "Are you serious, Mr. — I mean Coach — O'Shea? Anything goes?"

Danny smiled and nodded.

"Okay. I'm in!" Nubie exclaimed, then he frowned. "But I am not, repeat, not playing. Oh, and coach?"

"Yeah?"

"Do coaches get babes?"

•　•　•　•　•

Becky, Tad, Hanon, and Zolteck strolled down the sidewalk tossing a football between them. Their first practice was that afternoon, and they couldn't wait.

"It's gonna be awesome," said Zolteck.

"Yeah," said Becky

She looked up. They were passing a big, fancy-looking house. A taxi was pulled up to the curb beside it. Just then the door of the house popped open, and a man came tearing out of it. He was talking into a cellular phone. "Yeah, I'll be at the airport in fifteen minutes," he barked into the receiver. Then Becky noticed a boy standing behind the man. The boy was about her age.

"Hey, Dad, wait!" the boy shouted.

The man turned around. "I'll see you in a week, Johnny," he said. Then he leaped into the cab and it pulled away. The boy flopped down on the front steps of the house and sighed. He looked really upset. Becky felt sorry for him.

"Hey," she called. "You wanna play some football?"

The boy looked up. "Sure," he said.

"Great!" Becky replied. "Come on with us."

The boy started down the steps.

"What's your name?" Zolteck asked him.

"Johnny Vanero."

Hanon put out his hand. "Welcome to our team, Johnny Vanero," he said enthusiastically.

The group of kids continued down the street. All of a sudden, they spotted a short Asian kid in the vacant lot beside them. The short kid was kicking a football against the wall. WHOMP! The kids' mouths dropped open. The ball was going ballistic! Whoosh! It sailed through an open second-story window across the street.

The next thing they heard was a tremendous crash.

"My aquarium!" a man's voice shouted.

"Wow!" Becky stared at the short Asian kid in admiration. "What a kick!"

"Yeah," agreed Hanon. "That kid has killer feet, all right."

"He sure does," said Zolteck, with a worried look. "But I think . . . uh . . . we'd better get out of here!" He pointed up at the window. A man was leaning out of it, shaking his fist at them.

"You little creeps!" he hollered. "I'm calling the police. You can take your stupid football and —" The man slammed the ball down at them.

Becky caught it. "Yeah, you're right," she squinted up at the man's furious face. "He doesn't look like much of a football fan." She gave the kid a high-five. "Do you wanna play football?"

The Asian kid nodded. "You bet."

"Great! What's your name?"

"Marcus!" The kid grinned at her.

"Okay Marcus. Now, let's get out of here! We've got to meet my Dad out in front of the 7-11 so he can give us a ride out to the practice field."

• • • • •

When Becky and the others reached the 7-11 five minutes later, they found Danny talking to a small boy. The boy was dressed in a cowboy suit and sitting on the mechanical rocking horse by the door.

"Hey," Danny was saying to the kid. "You ever played football?"

The kid shook his head. "No."

"Well, do you like football?"

"No."

"Do you wanna play football?"

The kid in the cowboy hat just shrugged.

Becky tugged at Danny's sleeve. "Hey, Dad. Are you sure about this one?" she whispered.

"No," Danny whispered back. "But we need at least two more

players to have enough for a team." He raised his voice. "What's your name, kid?"

"Little Timmy Moore. I'm a cowboy."

"I can see that," Danny smiled. "Well, Timmy, like I said before, do you wanna play some football?"

Timmy Moore looked at him. "I already told you, NO."

Danny grinned. "Great," he said enthusiastically. "You can be on our team. Come on."

Becky groaned. "Dad," she muttered, "I hope you know what you're doing."

• • • • •

Danny threw open the door of the storage shed behind the gas station. "It's been kind of short notice," he said apologetically, "but I have managed to put together some equipment for you guys." He switched on the light. There was a pile of football equipment there, but . . . .

"Man, this stuff looks like it comes from prehistoric times," exclaimed Hanon.

"You ain't kiddin'," agreed Johnny Vanero, picking up a weird-looking pink and orange helmet. "Like it's what the dinosaurs wore when they played football."

"Come on," said Danny. "It's not that bad. Now, let's try to get you guys suited up so we can get out to the field."

"Okay," said the boys. Becky had already gone off to the gas station's ladies room to get dressed in her uniform. The boys stripped down to their underwear. Everyone turned to gawk at Tad, who was wearing bright pink boxer shorts.

"Hey, Tad, why are you wearing your sister's underwear?" Zolteck asked.

Tad turned as pink as his shorts. "Th-they're not my sister's," he stammered. "My Dad did the laundry this week."

"Oh," Zolteck said. The fat kid bent over and started digging through the pile for a jersey that would fit him. He didn't find one right away, but he did manage to make a duck's bill out of a pair of knee pads. He put it on.

"This is kind of cool," he announced. "How do I look? Quack! Quack! Quack!"

"Zolteck, cut the quacking," Hanon told him. "We're football players, remember? Not ducks!"

"Oh, yeah, right." Zolteck took off the beak.

Hanon tried on a pair of shoulder pads. They were so big his head disappeared in between them. "Somehow, I don't think this is my correct size," he drawled.

Danny looked at him and shook his head. "Here, try these." He dug another pair from the slowly shrinking pile of equipment.

Just then the door of the shed suddenly swung open.

"Yipes!" Zolteck shrieked. "It's a mom. Run for your lives!"

"Coach? Coach O'Shea?" A woman stepped inside, ignoring the boys who were frantically diving behind boxes and under old car parts to cover themselves up. "My name's Cheryl Berman. Could I talk to you for a moment?"

"Uh, sure."

"Its about my son, Jake." Mrs. Berman reached behind the door and yanked out a tiny eight-year-old boy. The kid was so pale, he looked almost blue. He was wearing glasses even thicker than Nubie's, and his ears stuck out from his head like Dumbo the elephant's. He also had a terrible cold.

"This is my son, Jake," Mrs. Berman said proudly. "He wants to be part of your team. I'm terribly sorry he's so late, but I had to take him to see Dr. Harding. See, Jake sneezed three times this morning. It had me worried sick. His allergies are awful. And you can't be too careful. He has asthma, too, see." The kids all turned to stare at Jake. He looked like a sick, underfed chicken. When Jake noticed them eyeing him, he sneezed again very, very loudly.

"As you can see," Mrs. Berman went on, "my poor Jakie is not very strong. In fact, he's been sickly his whole life. At birth, he only weighed one pound eleven ounces. I can show you pictures, Mr. O'Shea. It was enough to break your heart. He spent the first six months of his life in an incubator. Anyway, I think football is just the medicine for him."

Danny stared at the small boy, who stared solemnly back through his magnifying-glass glasses. "What do you say, Jake?"

The tiny boy shrugged. "My shrink told her I gotta get out more," he sniffed.

Tad couldn't help himself. He had never seen any living person as sickly-looking as this kid was. He stretched out one finger and poked Jake in the arm to make sure he was real.

Jake stared at him accusingly. "OWWWWW" he wailed, and started coughing. He didn't stop until Marcus reached out and slapped him on the back. Then he wailed "Owwwww!" again.

Hanon rolled his eyes. "I don't know about this guy."

"You remember what Coach said," Tad reminded him. "Everybody plays."

"Yeah, but . . . ."

The door to the storage shed burst open with a boom. There stood Becky in her uniform. Compared to Jake Berman she looked like the Terminator come to life. Everyone gaped at her, then started to cheer.

"All right, Icebox!"

"I'm ready," Becky announced grimly. "Come on, you guys. Let's get out there and kick some butt."

The members of the team threw on their helmets and followed her out to the dirt field behind Danny's gas station.

● ● ● ● ●

Meanwhile, across town in the Kevin O'Shea Football Field within the Urbania Town Park, Kevin was leading the Cowboy's first practice session. The field looked great. The grass was newly mowed, and the yard lines were freshly marked in chalk.

Kevin sternly watched a row of boys perform jumping jacks in perfect time. "Okay!" he bellowed. "Let's hear our fight song."

The boys paused for a breath and then sang out:

"*We are the Cowboys. We couldn't be prouder.*
If you can't hear us.
We'll yell a little louder.

We are the cowboys . . .
So get out of our way!
Or we'll . . . kick you in the head.
Realllly haaard . . . ."

As their voices wobbled on the last note, Assistant Coach Butz frowned. "Fight song could use some work."

Kevin sighed. "Yeah, tell me about it." He blew his whistle. "Okay, you slobs! Hit the ropes! Hut! Hut! Hut!"

The boys tore across the field to the obstacle course. They moved through it smoothly and confidently.

Butz smiled. Kevin smiled, too. But his smile became a frown again as soon as the boys came racing back over to him.

"What are you?" he roared. "A bunch of old ladies? That was pathetic. Line up for inspection."

The boys nervously got in line. Marching up and down in front of them, Kevin gave each of them the once-over. "Murphy, get a haircut!" he barked.

"Yes, Coach O'Shea, sir."

"Patterson. Clean your helmet. That thing's a disgrace!"

"Aye-aye, Coach O'Shea, sir."

Kevin abruptly stopped and sniffed the air. "Briggs?"

"Y-y-es, Coach O'Shea, sir?"

"What's that smell?"

"Old Spice, sir. My father uses it, sir! I thought it smelled . . . m-m-m-manly, sir!"

"Perfume," Kevin hollered, "on a football field?! I don't think so."

Briggs hung his head. "Yes, Coach O'Shea, sir."

Kevin moved on to the next player, Green. The boy looked up at him. His eyes widened, and his jaw began to quiver.

"What's wrong with you?" Kevin barked.

"I-I'm scared, sir!"

Kevin's face softened. "Of what, son?"

The boy gulped. "Of y-y-ou, sir."

Kevin turned away. He grinned at Butz and winked. Then he turned back to the boy. "Get over it," he growled.

"Y-y-es, Coach O'Shea, sir."

"All right," Kevin blew his whistle again. "I want you to go climb those ropes again. And this time, lemme see some sweat!"

The team started climbing, fast.

"Looking good, boss," Butz said.

"Yeah, Butz. What can I tell you? I'm a winner!"

• • • • •

"Okay-doke," Danny clapped his hands. "Let's try it one more time. And try to keep in time, all right?"

"Sure thing, Coach." The team started doing their jumping jacks. But not even the most generous observer could say they were keeping time. As one person finished a jumping jack, another started. It didn't help that Danny wasn't clapping his hands in time either.

"That's great," Danny said, trying to sound as if he meant it. "Now, let's sing our fight song!"

The kids started to sing in high, out-of-tune voices:

> *"I don't know, but I've been told,*
> *"Butz's teeth are green with mold!"*
>
> *"I say thank you, you say please."*
> *"Kevin smells like year-old cheese!"*

Danny winced as they hit the last note. "Sounds good," he said weakly. He gestured at the makeshift obstacle course of tires he'd thrown together at the muddiest end of the field. "Let's try the course, okay? See how fast we can get through it."

"You betcha, Coach."

Danny watched in dismay as the kids started through the course. Some of them were pretty fast but, except for Becky, none of them seemed to have any idea which way to go or why. Danny reached for his whistle, intending to blow it and bring them all back. But then he remembered he didn't have a whistle.

"Hey! That's enough for now!" he shouted instead. "Come out onto the field, and we'll review what the game is all about."

"Sure thing, Coach!"

The kids straggled back across the field and slowly lined up in front of him.

"Okay," Danny cleared his throat. "Now, football may seem complicated, and it is. So we're just gonna worry about the basics today like offense and defense —"

Tad Simpson raised his hand.

"Yes, Tad?"

"Uhhh. Which are we, Coach?"

"When can I score a touchdown?" piped up Zolteck.

"When do we get our jerseys?" asked Hanon.

"What's it all about?" said Nubie from the sidelines.

Danny stared at him. "What's what all about?"

"Life," came the reply.

"Yeah," said Johnny. "Why does my Dad ignore me?"

Danny was starting to feel overwhelmed. "One at a time," he said. "Now to start with your question, Tad, ..." But before he could get any further, there was a sudden, loud BANG, BANG, BANG! Everyone jumped, and Jake Berman turned blue. Danny turned to see Timmy Moore standing behind him, firing his cap gun. "Timmy! What are you doing?" he asked helplessly.

"Practicing my shooting," Timmy replied seriously. "But you'd better get me some more caps before the game."

"What for?"

"So I can shoot the bad guys."

"What bad guys?" asked Danny in confusion.

Timmy looked at him as if he were stupid. "The other team, of course," he explained. "How else are we supposed to stop 'em?" Danny groaned and bent over with his head in his hands.

Zolteck turned to Becky. "Hey, what's the matter with your Dad? He looks like he's getting sick."

"Oh, nothing," Becky replied. "He's just overreacting, that's all. Now come on, you guys. Hut! Hut! Hut!" She threw the ball in the air, and everyone shuffled after it.

CHAPTER FIVE

KEVIN SAT AT THE HEAD OF THE dinner table, watching his seven-year-old daughter, Priscilla, say Grace. "God bless family . . . friends . . . flowers . . . Nickelodeon . . . all the little kitties . . . Pez . . . Mr. Lorenzo, the school janitor . . . ."

Kevin groaned. "Priscilla, get on with it."

"And God bless Daddy's favorite sport," Priscilla finished.

"Amen. Baby, dig in," said Kevin lifting his fork.

His wife, Karen, passed him the mashed potatoes. "You know, Kevin, I still don't understand why you didn't pick Becky for your team."

Kevin's face darkened. "Yes, you do."

Karen frowned at him. "No. I don't. She *is* your niece and she's one of the best players out there. "

Kevin took a bite of his steak. "Honey, she's a girl!"

"Kevin!" Karen looked mad. "What's that got to do with it?

"Girls *don't* play football."

"Oh?" Karen's eyes narrowed. "Kevin, I hate to tell you this, but women have run countries, sat on the Supreme Court, and discovered radium. I mean, if we can do all of these things, I think we can play a little Peewee football."

Kevin guffawed. "Yeah, right. I'd love to see the dame who discovered radium take a hit from Bruce Smith."

"Kevin, you really are a Neanderthal. When I'm not home, do you sit around cave painting, or maybe making tools out of stone? Or do you just wolf down hunks of raw meat?"

Kevin didn't answer. Instead, he shut his eyes and slowly brought his fingers up to his temples. "Hey, wait a minute!"

Karen shouted at him. "What is it now?"

"I'm having a vision!"

"A what?"

"A vision. A vision of pink-cheeked, pony-tailed, all-American girls in pleated skirts. They're jumping up and down and screaming for my Cowboys!" Kevin opened his eyes. "I need pom-poms! I need team spirit! I need cheerleaders!"

Debbie jumped to her feet. "Yeah! You're a genius, Daddy."

Priscilla covered her face. "Oh, brother."

"Oh, brother, is right," said her mother.

• • • • •

Hanon, Zolteck, and Tad headed down the street toward the supermarket. As they passed the barber shop, they peered through the window on tiptoes. Inside, a group of old men were gathered around a chalkboard set against the back wall. On it was written: "Peewee Game Odds: Cowboys +40 over Dannyboys."

Hanon looked at Zolteck. "Dannyboys?!"

Zolteck shrugged. "I guess that's what they're gonna call us 'til we come up with a better name."

"Yeah, well, we should come up with another name soon. I mean, the Dannyboys?" Hanon shook his head. "And the Cowboys by forty points? I know we're a long shot, but . . . ."

"Don't let get it get to you," said Zolteck. "Have a Cheetoh or two, or three."

"Thanks, Zollie." Hanon helped himself. "What part of the supermarket are we supposed to meet the Icebox in again?"

"Frozen foods," replied Zolteck.

"Why frozen foods?" Tad asked, as the supermarket's automatic doors slid open.

"'Cause that's where the popsicles are!" replied Zolteck. The three headed inside. As they cruised down the aisles, Tad started to sing, "Puff the Magic Dragon lived by the sea . . . ."

"He kicked Cowboy butt in Urbania . . . " crooned Zolteck.

"On a team they called Peewee!" finished Hanon.

The three looked at one another and grinned.

"That's more like it, fellas," Hanon said. "We can't let 'em get to us."

"Right on!" Tad agreed wholeheartedly. Zolteck didn't say anything. He was busy staring at the shelf in front of him, with a glazed look in his eyes.

Hanon shook him. "Zolteck? Are you all right?"

"Wha? Oh, yeah. I'm fine. But look at that!" breathed Zolteck, pointing at a cereal box. "Chocolate Cookie Crisps. That's so cool! What a great idea! It's like a potato chip and a cookie all in one!"

"It sure is," Tad said. "Only, it's *my* idea. I had that idea last Halloween. I even wrote the company. I'm suing!"

"Tad," Hanon sighed. "Get a life."

A toilet roll sailed over their heads and landed in a shopping cart parked at the end of the aisle. "Woooow!" all three said as another toilet roll went zipping past. They tiptoed to the end of the aisle and peeked around the corner.

A blond, blue-eyed kid about their age was standing there, whipping toilet rolls across three aisles into the cart.

"What a throw!" said Hanon excitedly. Tad said nothing. He was still studying the box.

"Yeah," said Zolteck. "What a find."

"What a face," said a voice behind them.

Hanon and Zolteck whirled around. "Icebox?"

Becky's face turned bright pink. "Oh. Hi, guys. I thought I was supposed to meet you over in frozen foods."

"Yeah, but . . . ." Hanon gestured at the blonde kid as another toilet roll came whipping down the aisle. Without thinking, Hanon lifted up his hand. Thwock! He looked down in amazement. "Hey! I caught it! I caught something!"

"Yeah," the blonde kid came over. "Nice catch."

Hanon stared at him. "Nice arm. What's your name?"

"Junior Floyd."

"Cool. I'm Hanon."

"I'm Zolteck." Zolteck pointed at Tad. "And this here's —"

"I'm *suing*," Tad burst out. "I'm serious. This is outrageous!"

"Our friendly neighborhood nut-case, Tad Simpson. Just ignore him." Zolteck looked at Junior intently. "You're new here, right?"

Junior nodded. "Yeah. My Mom and I just moved to town. She grew up here, but she left after high school."

"Great!" exclaimed Zolteck. "You wanna play some football?"

Junior grinned. "You bet."

"All right!" Hanon gave him a high-five. "Let's see that arm again. Oh yeah, and this here is the Icebox." He turned to introduce Becky, but she had disappeared. "Icebox?"

Zolteck nudged him. "Over there, behind the cookie display."

Hanon's eyes widened. "Icebox?"

"Go away!" Becky hissed.

Junior smiled. "Don't be shy, guy. Show yourself."

There was a huge Kerblang! The tower of cookie boxes toppled over and behind it stood Becky, still wearing her football outfit. "Uh, hi." She looked at Junior and tried to smile. Then she turned to the others. "Hey, guys. I'm sorry. I gotta go, okay? I'm late for some . . . uh . . . urgent business." She fled down the aisle.

Hanon, Zolteck, and Tad stared after her. "Icebox?" Junior gave them a confused look. "Hey," he asked. "Why do you keep calling that girl Icebox?"

"You'll find out soon enough," Zolteck replied. "Here. Have a Cheetoh."

● ● ● ● ●

Becky sat by her father in the truck. "One more block. Here. Pull over. This is the house."

"Okay." Danny started to get out. Becky yanked him back. "Wait, wait!" She got a tissue and wiped off his face, then opened the glove compartment and pulled out a comb.

"Hey, I don't get it. What's the big deal?"

Becky groaned. "Dad, you never listen! He's cute. He's available. He's got a great arm. I want him on my team, okay?"

She leaned forward and dragged the comb through her father's hair. Danny tried to wriggle away. "Come on, Becky, stop. Wouldya just *quit it*?"

Suddenly, he turned around. "What do you mean, he's available?" he asked suspiciously.

"Oh, nothing," Becky said. "Come on. Let's go."

"Okay." Danny started up the walk to the house.

"Wait!" Becky yanked him back again. "*Please* don't tell any jokes, okay? You *can't* tell jokes, you *never* could tell jokes, so —"

"Becky!" Her father eyed her with concern. "This is so . . . *not* like you. What's going on? You got a crush on this guy?"

Becky's eyes flashed. "Get real, Dad," she said scornfully. "I'm the . . . Icebox, remember? The Icebox *crushes*. The Icebox does not get *crushed*."

All of a sudden, her hand flew up to her mouth. "I-don't-believe-it. THERE HE IS!" She gasped, pointing numbly up at the living room window. Junior Floyd was sitting there watching T.V.

Becky flattened herself against the wall of the house. Danny grinned. "Oh, yeah," he said. "Just the same old Icebox . . . ."

"Help!" Becky was losing it. "I can't go in there. I look like such a geek. And he's so gorgeous, and —"

"Hey, Becky," Danny's face softened, "cool out, okay? I'll be right there with you, every step of the way. We'll just go in and casually ask him to join the team and . . . ." Danny's eyes bugged out of his head. "Good grief! It's Patty Murphy — I mean Floyd!"

Danny gaped through the window at a grown-up Patty entering the room carrying a tray of milk and cookies. Her heart-shaped locket glistened in the afternoon sunlight as she sat down on the couch beside her son.

Danny flattened himself against the wall beside Becky.

"Y-you didn't tell me his last name was Floyd!" he hissed.

"I did, too!" Becky retorted.

"You kept calling him Pretty Boy Floyd. Pretty Boy Floyd, you said. You didn't say anything about his mother being Patty Floyd!"

"What's the *difference?*"

"The *difference* is I used to know her, okay? When we were kids. She was a tweet, I mean, a sweet kid. I really biked — I mean, I really liked her and . . . ."

"Daddy! Would you get a grip?"

"Look who's talking."

The two of them stared at each other. At last, Danny took a deep breath. "Look," he said firmly, "one of us has got to knock on that door, and you're —"

Becky swallowed. "Here's the thing, Daddy," she interrupted him. "I'm TEN. That means I'm a lot younger than you. And I'm a lot more scared than you are. I'm just a *kid*, remember? I mean, I still sleep with a nite lite on . . . ."

"So do I!"

"Daddy, this is no time for bad jokes. We *need* a quarterback. I'm doing this for your own good." Becky leaped up, rang the doorbell, and raced away down the street.

Danny scowled at her. "Traitor!" he muttered.

Footsteps were approaching the door. "Hi . . . can I help you?" Patty started to say when she suddenly recognized him. "Danny?" A smile spread over her face. "Danny O'Shea! How are you?"

Patty's smile made Danny feel as if he were still in the fourth grade. He turned red. "Great!" he stammered.

"Well, come on in."

Danny stumbled over the doorstep. "Okay. Good idea. Sure thing, Fatty . . . I mean . . . Patty."

Danny sat on the couch watching Patty come across the room with a tray of lemonade. He knew he should help her, but also knew that he was so nervous that if he did, it would probably lead to disaster.

"So anyway," Patty was saying, "after my divorce I woke up one morning, looked out the window and said, why am I still here? I hate New York . . . ." Patty set down the tray and sat down beside Danny. " . . . so I came home." She finished with a smile.

Danny swallowed. "I know exactly what you mean," he said.

Patty looked confused. "Huh?"

"I mean about coming home."

Patty's face brightened. "Really? You moved away from Urbania, too?"

Danny coughed. "No — not exactly. But I visited Akron . . . once." Patty was looking at him like he was crazy. Danny decided he better change the subject fast. "So, what do you think about Junior joining our football team?"

"I don't know," Patty replied slowly. "I'm just not crazy about competitive sports for kids. I mean, it always comes down to the parents, doesn't it?"

"The parents?" said Danny. "I don't know —"

" . . . A bunch of middle-aged guys," Patty went on, "using innocent kids to work out their own childhood resentments."

Danny gazed at her in shock. Was that what he and Kevin were doing?

"Besides, I gotta tell you, you never struck me as the football coach type, Danny," Patty went on. "Not like Kevin . . . ."

Danny wiped his forehead. "Oh, but I am," he said.

"You're as competitive as your brother?" Patty asked, an amused look in her eyes.

"Oh . . . well . . . yeah, sure. I guess."

Patty shook her head. "Oh, Danny. I was about to say yes. Now, I'm not so sure."

Danny sighed. This wasn't going the way he wanted it to go at all. He glanced over at Patty. Didn't she want him to be like Kevin? All his life everyone had wanted him to be like Kevin. But Patty seemed to be saying she didn't. Danny took a deep breath.

"Look, Patty," he said. "I'm not interested in winning or saying anyone's better than anyone else. I just want a chance." He looked over at Patty again, and her eyes met his. "I mean for the kids," Danny finished.

Patty smiled. "Good for you, Danny," she said softly. "Junior can play for you — but under one condition . . . ." She winked at him. "You run those Cowboys out of town."

CHAPTER SIX

THE FOOTBALL FIELD BEHIND

Danny's gas station was buzzing with activity. A group of parents were gathered on the sidelines shouting encouragement to the kids out on the field.

"Hey, Tad!" Tad Simpson's father held up a brand-new Polaroid camera. "Say Super Bowl."

Marcus turned to Johnny. "I don't know what it is, but Dads really get into this. Mine had me up all night playing catch."

Johnny looked uncomfortable. "Yeah, I know," he mumbled. "My Dad was gonna come to practice today, but stuff came up. He's definitely coming tomorrow, though."

Danny gave a toot on his brand new whistle. "Okay, let's try some passing and catching." Junior jogged down to the end of the field and started firing passes.

Danny, Zolteck, Tad, and Nubie watched in amazement.

"Man, that guy's awesome!" said Zolteck.

"I can't believe you started without me!" wailed a high, squeaky voice behind them. It was Jake Berman. At least, the voice was Jake Berman's. But it was hard to tell exactly who the figure was waddling towards them. Covered from head to toe in thick foam rubber, it looked like the Michelin Man come to life.

"Jake, is that you?" Danny asked cautiously.

"Yup." Jake peered up at him from under his helmet. "My mom says the pads you gave me weren't enough."

Danny nodded. "Okay, Jake. Out on the field."

Jake waddled across the grass. The other kids ran up to surround him. "Hey, it's a life-size rubber ball."

"No, it's foam-rubber man!" Marcus gave Jake a slight push. He fell over and bounced up again like a blow-up toy clown. "Cool!" everyone said. They pushed Jake from person to person, letting him bounce off from each one of them in turn.

"This is great!" Jake squealed. "I don't feel a thing!" At that exact moment, he banged his head against the practice field's center post. Bonk! He fell backward onto the grass.

"My BABY!" Cheryl Berman shrieked. "You've killed my baby!"

Jake groggily lifted his head. "It's okay, Ma," he said weakly. "I'm not dead yet."

"We've got to get you home at once."

"Uh-uh," Jake shook his head stubbornly. "I don't wanna. I wanna keep playing. I'm having fun."

"That-a-boy, Jake" said Danny, helping him to his feet. "Now, everybody, why don't we try getting into a huddle!"

The kids formed a ragged group at mid-field.

"Okay, guys," Danny said. "We've been playing together for a few days now, and we're starting to learn something about football, right?"

"Right!" came the hearty reply.

"And one thing we're learning is that communication is key. I signal the play to the quarterback, and he gives it to you in the huddle. Then you'll try to execute the play in the field —"

"What does execute mean?" wondered Marcus.

"Do it," said Zolteck.

"Right. Any more questions? Good. Let's give it a try." Danny headed back to the sideline.

The kids all turned to Junior — except for Zolteck. He was facing the opposite way, his hand cupped around his ear as though he were listening for something. "Could it be?" His eyes lit up. "Hey, it's the Good Humor Man!"

"Zolteck!" Junior tugged him by the ear. "This is a huddle, remember? We're not out here to listen for ice cream trucks."

Reluctantly, Zolteck turned to face the group again. From the sideline, Danny went through an elaborate series of gestures, describing the play.

"Okay," Junior nodded crisply. "That's a curl out to the flanker. On two," he pointed at Hanon.

"It's no fair," whined Jake. "How come they never call a play for me?"

"You're a tackle, diphead," Hanon said.

"Hey," Jake puffed himself up in his Michelin Man costume. "No one calls me diphead, except my sister."

"Look," Tad sighed. "I'll settle this. I'll run the ball."

"Why can't I run the ball?" grumbled Marcus.

"'Cause you're slow and no one likes you?" suggested Hanon.

From the sidelines Danny made a "hurry-up!" gesture.

"Says who?" demanded Marcus angrily.

"Says me!" declared Jake.

"Well, you can't come to my party," said Marcus.

"What party?" demanded Zolteck. "No one said anything to me about no party."

"That's 'cause you'd eat all the food," said Hanon.

"Guys, come on," said Becky impatiently.

Now the entire huddle was breaking up into a wall of name-calling. Junior threw up his arms and strode off the field. After a moment, Becky followed him. She walked over to Danny, who was watching in dismay from the sideline.

"Diphead!" bellowed Zolteck.

"Dork!" retorted Hanon.

"Oh, boy," Danny shook his head. "I don't know about this, Beck'."

"Don't worry, Dad," Becky replied. "I mean, we're definitely making progress. It's just going to take a while that's all."

Danny blew his whistle. "Okay, guys," he said wearily. "Let's take it from the top. Huddle!"

• • • • •

Kevin stood in the center of his study. A single spot lamp was focused on a mattress propped up by Karen on one side and Murphy and Briggs on the other. Pinned to the center of the mattress was a life-size cardboard cutout of Becky.

Karen poked her head out from behind the mattress. "I can't believe I'm contributing to this," she groaned.

"Don't worry about it, honey," replied Kevin. He turned to Patterson, who was standing in front of the mattress dressed in a helmet and shoulder pads.

"Okay," he barked. "Assume the three-point position." Patterson leaned forward with a menacing growl.

"Now," Kevin gestured at the cut-out of Becky. "This is your opponent, Patterson. Whatever it takes, you must defeat her."

Karen snorted. "That's good. Put Patterson in therapy for years and years . . . ."

Kevin glared at his wife. "Karen, please. It's nothing personal, we're just trying to get ready for the big game." He turned to Patterson again. "Remember, Becky's all they got! Hit her low and don't let go! Okay. Hut! Hut! Hut! Go!"

Patterson lunged forward. He rammed into the mattress and bounced off. Kevin shook his head. "You need practice, son," he sighed. "Stand back and take a lesson from the master."

Kevin took Patterson's place. Karen looked on nervously. "Honey, are you sure about this?"

"Just hold the mattress, babe! Briggs, you count off."

"Yes, Coach O'Shea, sir. Hut! Hut! Hut!"

On the third "Hut!" Kevin plowed forward like a raging bull. As he slammed into the mattress, Karen screamed and let go. "Agghhhh!" Kevin drove the mattress across the room and crashed through the window. Shattered glass flew everywhere.

"Help! Help!"

Karen and the boys raced to the window. Kevin and the mattress were tangled up in the branches of the oak tree just outside. Kevin was hanging on for dear life. "Don't just stand there, do something!" he howled up at them.

"Oh, honey! Don't worry! Hang on!" Karen raced to the phone and dialed frantically. "Fire Department? Yes. We have an emergency at Kevin O'Shea's house! Can you get over here right away? My husband's caught up in a tree!"

• • • • •

Priscilla rewound the VCR as Karen and Debbie looked on. Kevin was watching from his favorite armchair. His leg was wrapped in an ace bandage, and he was holding a pair of crutches. "Do we have to watch that thing again?" he grumbled as his "tackle" was replayed yet again on the wide-screen TV.

"Just consider it as preparation for the big game, honey," Karen told him, with a grin.

Kevin turned to Debbie. "I get no respect," he complained. "Anyway, the point is that Becky's the only decent player they've got. If we neutralize her, we've got the game in our pocket."

"I know, Daddy," Debbie said. "You already told me. Anyway, Becky's not their only decent player. What about Junior?"

Kevin sat up in his chair. "Who?"

Debbie's eyes misted over. "Junior," she repeated dreamily. "You know, Junior Floyd? El Hunko?"

"El What?" said Kevin. "Watch your language, Debbie! Who the heck is this Junior character?"

"Don't you know?" Karen said, needling him. "Junior Floyd. Danny's new quarterback? I hear he's got a great arm."

• • • • •

Kevin's eyes widened in alarm.

CHAPTER SEVEN

NUBIE STOOD BESIDE DANNY
watching the team practice. He could hardly believe it, but they were actually seeing some improvement.

Out on the field, Junior handed the ball off to Becky. Zolteck and Johnny tried to block her, but the Icebox was unstoppable. The team burst into applause as she crossed the touchdown line.

"Way to go!" Nubie shouted, then broke off. What was he doing shouting like a dumb sports fan? "I hate football!" he reminded himself. Just then, something in the weeds across the field caught his eye. The sunlight was reflecting off from binoculars!

He picked up his own binoculars and peered through them. Over in the weeds was none other than Coach Kevin O'Shea and beside him was Assistant Coach Butz!

Nubie put down the binoculars and hustled over to Danny. "Spies!" he hissed dramatically. "In the weeds."

Danny grabbed Nubie's binoculars and squinted into them. "Of all the low-down, nasty tricks. If Kevin and Butz think they can get away with this, they've got another think coming."

Danny thrust the binoculars back into Nubie's hands and strode across the field to the gas station.

"Hey, guys," Nubie shouted. "Urgent team meeting."

"Hooray," Zolteck raced off the field. "Now I can get a snack."

Moments later, the team clustered around the phone booth outside the gas station. Danny was inside the booth.

"State police?" Danny squawked into the phone in a high-pitched old lady's voice. "Why, thank goodness. This is Thelma May Rogers, and I'm 86 years old, dag nab it. I live right across from the Sunoco in Urbania . . . and there's two strange men hiding in the bushes spying on some kids. I'm sorry, but I don't think it's right for grown men to parade around in their underwear like that!"

The kids collapsed in hysterics as Danny hung up.

Junior turned to Becky. "I didn't think so at first . . . but your dad's cool."

Becky shrugged. "Yeah . . . ." She grinned at Danny.

• • • • •

A siren sounded in the distance. It rapidly drew closer, but Kevin and Butz paid no attention. They were too busy watching Danny and the kids through his binoculars. "Team meeting, huh?" Kevin said.

"They're just standing around that phone booth." Butz squawked. "What the heck are they waiting for?"

A voice behind them suddenly shouted, "Freeze!" Kevin and Butz both whirled around. Five cops were standing there with their guns drawn.

"W-what's this all about, officers?" Kevin stammered.

"You guys," came the reply. "You're both under arrest!"

• • • • •

Danny and the kids watched gleefully through Nubie's binoculars as a very angry Kevin and an indignant Butz were led over to the police car in handcuffs and driven away.

"You know what this means, guys?" Danny asked solemnly.

"No," everyone shouted at once.

"It means they're starting to get scared, fellas. It means that . . . we're for real!"

• • • • •

Danny, the team members, and their parents sat in Danny's dark living room. Suddenly, flashlights started swirling through the room like spotlights, and dramatic music came booming out of the speakers on either side of the couch. It was the theme from the movie "2001." One of the flashlights — held by Mr. Zolteck — fixed on Danny, who was standing in the front of the room holding a "Mr. Microphone."

Danny cleared his throat. "Since the dawn of man," he began in a hushed, solemn voice, "there have been two key ingredients necessary to civilized life: Food and football. Yes, through the years, there have many great football teams — none of which I can think of at the moment. But now a new team has formed, each individual scientifically selected. A team so bad, so awesome, that when you see them you're gonna go 'WHOA!'"

"Whoa!" shouted all the parents.

"That's right, sports fans," Danny intoned, flicking on the flashlight in his hand and focusing it on a giant paper-covered hoop behind him. "If there's gonna be Peewee football in Urbania, *everybody's going to play*. SO HOW ABOUT A BIG HAND FOR . . . ."

Danny reached up and tore the paper from the hoop, revealing the football-shaped banner beneath spray-painted with the words, "THE LITTLE GIANTS!!!"

The room exploded into cheers as Becky came leaping through the hoop wearing her silver-and-black skull-and-crossbones helmet.

"She's buff, she's bad, she's beautiful," Danny declared. "Let's hear it for Becky 'The Icebox' O'Shea." Hanon came jumping through the hoop behind her. "He's fast, he's furious, he's fabulous. Rasheed 'Hot Hands' Hanon." The room rocked with applause. "And next up, our very own lethal weapon, Rudy 'The Cheese Man' Zolteck." Zolteck congaed his way in to the room.

Mr. Zolteck frowned and turned to his wife. "The Cheese Man?" he asked. "I don't get it."

"Think about it, sweetheart," replied Mrs. Zolteck.

There was a loud crunch as Zolteck chowed down on a Cheetoh. Mr. Zolteck smiled. "Oh yeah," he said. "The Cheese Man. Of course! That's my boy!"

"And that's not all," Danny yelled over the cheers. "Here's our next star player. Timmy 'I Wanna Score' Moore." Timmy came out in his cowboy costume, his cap guns blazing.

"Rope 'em in, son," shouted his father.

"Now, Jake, 'Michelin Man' Berman."

Cheryl Berman shrieked and fell to the floor in a faint.

"Marcus 'Kick 'em High' Chin."

"Yeah!" His parents, who had been quiet up until this moment, screamed so loud the ceiling shook.

"Tad 'The Snake' Simpson."

"Thatta boy!" Tad's father was so excited, he jumped up and tumbled headfirst over the coffee table.

"Johnny 'The Viper' Vanero."

Everyone looked around, but Johnny's parents were nowhere to be seen. Johnny hung his head. "My Dad said he was coming," he mumbled, then he smiled shyly as the room rocked with still more applause.

"And last but not least," said Danny quietly. "Our newest player, and I don't need to tell you we couldn't do it without him, our quarterback, Junior 'Pretty Boy' Floyd." The other kids joined in the cheers as Junior ambled through the loop, a football under his arm. Patty smiled proudly.

"Ladies and gentlemen, THE LITTLE GIANTS!"

● ● ● ● ●

Danny followed his guests to the door. As he went, he glanced over at the food table. It looked like an army had swept over it. Everything — even the anchovy pizza Becky had ordered so they'd be sure to have some leftovers — had been demolished, mostly by Zolteck.

"Hey, Coach," Zolteck grinned up him. "Good party. *Excellent* food."

"Quite a spread," agreed Mr. Zolteck.

"Yes," piped up Mrs. Zolteck, wiping a tear from her eye. "You're a saint, Coach O'Shea! A saint!"

"I don't know about you being a saint," added Hanon. "But goodnight, my man. Cool party."

"Yes, it sure was fun," cried his father, enthusiastically shaking Danny's hand. The two families exited down the front steps. Johnny Vanero slipped out behind them.

"G'night Coach," he said quickly.

"Hey, Johnny," Danny pulled him back. "I thought I was going to meet your dad tonight."

Johnny stared down at his tennis shoes. "He's got business and stuff. See ya." He skipped hastily down the stairs. Danny stared after him.

"Hey, Coach?" Danny started. It was Junior and Patty Floyd. "Uh . . . yeah, Junior?"

"Your onion dip sucked, but bottom line?" Junior grinned. "You're okay, Coach O'Shea."

"Thanks, Junior." Danny blushed.

"And, uh, could you get me your brother's autograph?"

"Junior!" Patty shoved him out the door.

Patty looked at Danny and smiled. "I don't know how to thank you, Danny. This was such a blast."

"Well . . . it was nothing."

"You're really doing an amazing job with the kids. All that time I knew you, I had no idea you would be like this."

"Well, I was eleven," Danny said modestly. "I've probably changed quite a bit."

"I guess you're right." Patty frowned. "Have I changed?"

"Well, you're taller. Plus you can drive now. But to be honest," Danny took a deep breath, "your face is exactly how I remember it."

"Ma, come on," Junior called.

"Well, good night, Danny." Patty went out the door.

● ● ● ● ●

Kevin sat in his study brooding. The room was a shrine to his football career. The walls were lined with plaques and banners and trophies. But Kevin ignored them all. Instead, he stared up at the newspaper headline pinned above his desk. "GIANTS END O'SHEA'S CAREER," it said in thick black letters. "PROMISING ROOKIE BLOWS OUT KNEE."

"Grrrrr," Kevin growled at the headline.

The door swung open. Karen walked in carrying a tray with a roast beef sandwich and a glass of milk on it. She set the tray on the desk and bowed.

"Here is your sandwich, oh mighty one."

"Quit makin' fun of me," snapped Kevin. "Who would believe it? ME! Arrested — handcuffed! Humiliated! And by my own brother."

"Well, how do you think I feel?" Karen asked. "Married to a Peeping Tom —"

"I've really got to hand it to him," Kevin went on. "Calling the State cops instead of the locals. What a brilliant move! But don't worry. I'm gonna get him back for this . . . ."

Karen shook her head at him. "Kevin, it's Peewee football, remember? It's supposed to be fun."

"Fun!" Kevin exploded. "This isn't fun, honey. This is WAR! And if it's WAR my baby brother wants, then it's WAR he's gonna get!"

"I wish you'd calm down," Karen said. "I still don't see why you can't just have one team."

"One team," Kevin said angrily. "Don't you understand? This town depends on Kevin O'Shea to *win*. People don't buy Chevys from losers. And I'm a winner. That's what I am. Kevin O'Shea — a winner! You got that?" he glared at her.

Karen bowed. "Whatever you say, oh mighty one."

Behind her Kevin just growled.

CHAPTER EIGHT

THE COWBOYS WERE RUNNING A drill, carrying footballs through a row of cones. "Murphy!" Kevin called. "You're holding that ball like a loaf of bread. Okay, let's try it again. Come on, HUSTLE!"

This time it went better. "Not bad, boss," said Butz.

"No, not too bad, but what's this I hear about Marvin changing the odds down at the barber shop?"

Butz hesitated. "Yeah, well, they did change the odds. But they still got us down as the winners. Only instead of putting us ahead by 40 points, they got us ahead by 12."

"Twelve?" Kevin was enraged. "Do they think a team coached by my lamebrained baby brother could come within 12 points of my Cowboys?"

Kevin raised the whistle to his lips and blew. "What are you guys doing out there?" he yelled. "This ain't no picnic. This is football — FOOTBALL! Now, lemme see some sweat!"

● ● ● ● ●

Danny and Nubie looked on as Junior whipped a pass to Hanon. Hanon speared it with one hand. But when he turned his hand over to let go, the ball still stuck to it. "Hey! What's going on?"

Everyone turned to look at Zolteck, who was holding a large can of glue. "What d'ya think, Coach?" Zolteck wriggled his eyebrows. "Works pretty good, huh?"

Nubie answered for Danny. "No, Zolteck. I don't think so."

"Hey!" Hanon was still flapping his hand up and down. "Someone get over here and get this thing offa my hand!"

"Coming," sighed Danny. Hanon's hand was covered with so much glue that washing it off was going to be a big chore. Still, the

Little Giants were making progress. Hanon was starting to catch. Zolteck had made it through the obstacle course once. And even Tad Simpson could run to the forty-yard line without tripping over his own shoelaces.

Kevin must be getting nervous now, Danny thought. He glanced down the field. Junior had the ball and Becky was going after him. Crunch! The Icebox made another brilliant tackle. Danny wondered if she still had a crush on Junior.

"She does," Nubie said behind him.

"How did you know what I was thinking?"

"I occasionally try my hand at mind reading," Nubie replied modestly.

"Ah, I see."

"Anyhow, Coach, it's almost noon and —"

Danny slapped his forehead. "Oh, yeah! How could I forget? The team car wash is this afternoon, right?"

• • • • •

The scene outside of Danny's gas station looked more like a party than a car wash. Sure, there was a row of dirty cars lined up behind the sign that read: "CAR WASH $1.00 - HELP URBANIA'S OWN LITTLE GIANTS RAISE MONEY FOR OUR JERSEYS," and everywhere you looked kids were spraying hoses and wielding squeegees. But there was also loud dance music blaring out of Becky's boombox. And as they washed cars, the kids and their parents were singing, dancing, and generally getting down.

Becky hosed down a station wagon parked in front of her. Suddenly, she looked up and froze. Junior was chasing her cousin, Debbie, with a hose. Debbie seemed to be enjoying it.

"Wow, Beck," Debbie ran over to her. "I'm so jealous of you. Being in the huddle with Junior Floyd . . . . Even the twelve-year-old girls at school think he's a fox . . . ."

"Oh," Becky said coldly. "I don't really notice."

A car horn honked behind them. "Debbie, come on. We gotta go!" Karen called.

"Coming," Debbie smiled. "See ya, Icebox." She winked.

Becky groaned. "I think I'm going to be sick."

Zolteck eyed her with concern. "I don't know, Icebox, maybe you should become a cheerleader."

"Are you kidding?" Becky said. "Cheerleading's for girls."

• • • • •

Becky pulled the blue angora sweater over her head and carefully outlined her mouth in the pink lipstick she'd bought at the supermarket. Then she pinned her hair on top of her head and peered at herself in the mirror. She studied herself a moment, then mimed a cheer. "Give me a G, give me an I . . . ."

Just then she heard the front door downstairs opening. Becky quickly unpinned her hair, wiped the lipstick off her face, and pulled her regular sweatshirt on over the pretty sweater.

"Hey, Beck." Danny walked in the room. "I've got an idea for a whole new defense!"

"Dad," Becky cut him off with a look.

"Yeah?"

"Uh . . . what do boys like better: if you act that pretty-dumb girl way or if you have a mean tackle?"

Danny blinked at her. "You got me, sweetheart. But any boy worth knowing likes you for being just what you are."

"Well . . . maybe," Becky said doubtfully. "But Uncle Kevin says that if you're too good at sports, you end up toothless, single, and bald."

"Yeah, well, your Uncle Kevin's a Neanderthal." Danny glanced over at Becky and raised his eyebrows. "Hey! Are you wearing lipstick?"

Becky hastily shook her head. "Naah, Dad. I just ate a cherry Tootsie Pop."

"Oh. Well, anyway, back to this defense. See, we want to use you as our key offensive element."

"Uh, Dad?"

"Yes, honey?"

"Could we please talk about this later? I'm kind of tired right now." Becky flopped back on her bed and closed her eyes.

CHAPTER NINE

BUTZ WAS HOSING DOWN THE CARS,
so Kevin answered the phone. "O'Shea Chevrolet!" The voice of
Orville from the Coffee Cup came barking loudly out of the
receiver. "Mr. O'Shea. "*Kevin* O'Shea?!"

"Yeah, Orville, that's my name. What's up?"

"Kevin! Great! I got a hot tip for you. A family just moved
into town, and they've got this ten-year-old kid named Spike. Let
me put it to you this way: Do the words 'born to play football'
mean anything to you?"

Kevin pulled the phone back to his ear and listened very
closely to the rest of what Orville had to say. A few minutes later,
he hung up the phone. "Whoo-ee!" Bounding to his feet, Kevin
reached for his jacket.

"Hey, Butz, take care of the shop," he shouted. "I've got some
urgent *football* business." Jumping into his Corvette, Kevin zoomed
out of the lot.

● ● ● ● ●

At the same exact moment Danny was also receiving an
unexpected phone call. "Danny? Danny O'Shea?" croaked the
voice of Orville's brother, Wilbur. "Great! Have I got some big
news for you. New family in town, capiche? They've got a tough
little ten-year-old kid — a monster! His name's Spike, and from
what I hear, his middle name is Football."

Danny leaped up and raced out of the gas station office. "Oh,
no!" His old red truck had a tow attached to it with a broken-down
Plymouth at the end of it. Just then Danny noticed Becky over by
the gas pumps, filling up her go-cart.

"Becky!" he pushed her aside. "I need the go-cart. Now!"

"Hey, Daddy, what's going on?"

"No time to explain." Danny yanked the gas hose out of the go-cart. Picking up Becky's helmet from the hood, he leaped into the front seat.

"But Dad —"

"No time . . . ."

Danny took off in a cloud of dust.

● ● ● ● ●

Danny fumed waiting for the red light to change. Suddenly, he noticed a gleaming red Corvette pulling up beside him. It was Kevin! And he was grinning. Danny tooted on his horn.

"Hey, Kev," he sang out. "Where you going?"

Kevin's grin disappeared. "Oh, just out for a little spin." He glanced down at Danny. "What's with the go-cart?"

Danny shrugged. "Nothing. Becky just asked me to check the compression."

The light turned green. Brrr! Riiip! They roared off. Kevin drew ahead, but Danny floored it and managed to catch up.

"Is there some reason you're following me, Danny?" Kevin had to shout to be heard over the warring engines.

"No," Danny shouted back. "Just haven't been out for a drive in a while." He smiled. "Thought we'd enjoy it together!"

Kevin grimaced. "He's MINE!" he shrieked.

Zoom. Zip. The two of them sped along neck and neck down Main Street. Old ladies dropped their packages and parcels. Shopkeepers came running out of their stores to watch the race. But Kevin and Danny didn't notice.

"This whole town may love you, Kevin," Danny was yelling. "But I know what a jerk you truly are. When we were kids, you treated me like dirt!"

"That's a lie! I treated you like a prince."

"You ignored me!"

Danny hit the brakes just in time to make the red light at the end of Main Street. But Kevin just flashed a grin at the cop and whizzed on through. The cop threw his hat on the ground.

Danny thumped the steering wheel. Kevin was going to beat him again — or was he? Danny glanced over at the empty playing field on his left. Turning the go-cart steering wheel, Danny sped diagonally across the field. The go-cart bucked like a wild bronco. Danny zoomed across the field, over the sidewalk, off the curb, and back onto the road again. He checked his rearview mirror. Kevin was half a block behind him.

"Way to go!" Danny cheered, but Kevin came whipping up behind him. Kevin was flooring it. Splash! Danny hit a puddle and almost spun out of control, but he straightened out just in time. The two brothers tore along neck and neck.

A whistle sounded up ahead. They were nearing the train crossing. Kevin gunned the engine, determined to get there ahead of the train. But the arm came down with a clang. Too late! He hit the brakes. But Danny in the go-cart streaked underneath the arm and across the train tracks, seconds ahead of the train!

"You little rat!" Kevin shook his fist out the window. But Danny was gone and the train was chugging along in front of him. There was nothing he could do.

● ● ● ● ●

Danny pulled up to the ordinary-looking suburban ranch-style house and stepped out of the go-cart. The front yard of the house was littered with furniture and boxes. A man was standing in the center of it. A *huge* man.

Danny stood up as tall as he could. "Uh, excuse me," he said, making his voice a whole octave deeper. "Are you . . . "

The man stuck out an enormous hand. "Don't tell me," he cried enthusiastically. "Coach O'Shea!"

"Uh . . . Yeah. I'm Coach O'Shea."

Mr. Hammersmith struck a pose like the figure on the Heisman Trophy. "Who am I?" he demanded.

Danny gulped. "You remember my playing days, huh?"

"Remember 'em?" Mr. Hammersmith boomed. "I treasure 'em!" "Uh . . . great." said Danny. "Now, where's —"

"Spike. His name's Spike. And he's right over there."

Mr. Hammersmith pointed at the porch steps. A boy was climbing them with a refrigerator strapped to his back. Danny's eyes almost bugged out of his head. This was Spike? He was the biggest, baddest-looking ten-year-old, Danny had ever seen. The kid looked like he was made of solid steel. Even his ears looked like they could inflict serious damage.

"Keep cool!" Danny mumbled to himself. "Just keep cool."

"Hey, Spike," Mr. Hammersmith shouted. "Come on over here and meet Coach O'Shea."

Spike dropped the refrigerator with a ka-bang and thundered over, stretching out his hand.

"Go on, Coach, shake his hand. He won't bite."

Danny took Spike's hand. Owww! A bonecrusher!

"So you like football, son?" he yelped, barely remembering to keep his voice deep.

"Like football?" bellowed Mr. Hammersmith. "Spike was born for football! Look at him, O'Shea. First skin he ever touched was pigskin. By the time he was four months old, Spike could push a football across the floor with his head." At 18 months he did his first one-arm pull-up. He turned to Spike. "Give me ten, Son."

Danny gasped as Mr. Hammersmith held out his muscular arm. Spike did ten one-armed pull-ups in less than a minute.

"He's quite a . . . boy." Danny forgot to make his voice deep.

"You betcha," growled Mr. Hammersmith. He pulled a ball from behind his back.

"Now, fumble!"

Spike dived on the ball like a wild dog after a bone.

Danny shook his head in awe. Hammersmith shot him a suspicious look. "For a football star, you seem kinda small . . . ."

Danny winked at him. "That's just what they thought."

He breathed a heartfelt sigh of relief as Mr. Hammersmith smiled and winked back. Spike was his!

• • • • •

Nubie crouched down over the handmade "Hypnosis Wheel" and gave it a spin. "See," he said, glancing over at Hanon, who was watching the rainbow-colored blur with wide eyes. "I can give Hanon a posthypnotic suggestion that will make him catch every pass thrown to him!"

Junior shook his head. "You really think this is gonna work?"

"It's worth a try," Nubie said. "I just hope it doesn't turn him into a chicken!"

"A chicken?!" Hanon's head popped up.

They heard Danny blowing his whistle. "Guys! Great news. We have a new player." Danny strode out on to the field. Spike was beside him.

The members of the Little Giants all stared. This was their new player? He made Zolteck look small.

"Who is that guy?" breathed Zolteck.

Tad's face was green. "He looks like a side of beef."

"Or a genetics experiment gone terribly wrong," said Nubie.

Spike stared back at them. He didn't seem very impressed. On the contrary, he looked disgusted. The Little Giants looked down at themselves. Zolteck was covered with Cheetoh crumbs as usual. Timmy Moore was playing with his cap guns. Tad Simpson was dressed in clothes that clashed, and Jake Berman was in the middle of one of his nine-hundred daily asthma attacks. Maybe Spike was right. They weren't the most impressive-looking team in the world.

They turned to Spike again, looking at him almost pleadingly this time. Spike shook his head. "Spike's in trouble," he announced in a monotone voice. "Spike sees a Peewee disaster."

"Okay, kids!" Danny blew his whistle. "Spike here's gonna be our new tailback."

"Great!" Nubie showed the first signs of enthusiasm. "Now we can run that brilliant new play of mine. The Annexation of Puerto Rico."

Spike scowled. "What's the Annexation of Puerto Rico?"

Nubie beamed. "Quite possibly the greatest offensive play ever conceived," he replied. "See, it —"

"Hey, Nubie," Danny cut him off. "I don't think we're ready for that yet." He turned to Spike. "Now, what formation do you like to run out of, Spike?" he asked eagerly.

"Power One," Spike boomed. "Who's Spike's lead blocker?"

"The Icebox!" everyone chanted.

"Where's he at?"

Becky raised her hand. "Right here."

Spike folded his monstrous arms across his mammoth chest. "Spike don't play with girls," he growled.

Becky shoved a football in Spike's gut. "Oh, yeah?" she hissed. "Well, I can tackle anything, any time, anywhere."

Spike looked at her. "Listen, you beserko Barbie doll, you mess with Spike, you mess with death!"

Becky snorted. "Yeah. You talk the talk, but can you walk the walk?"

"Try me." Spike leaned toward her.

Becky leaned toward him. "I will."

Spike made his huge hand into a fist. "Let's go."

"Right now." Becky made her hand into a fist.

"Uh-oh," said Hanon. "Looks like we're going to see blood!"

"Somebody call 911!" squealed Jake Berman.

Danny shoved his way in between Spike and Becky. "Okay, that's enough. Hold it. Hold it!"

A ding! ding! came from the gas station. Everyone turned to look. A jeep had pulled up for service.

"Hey, Beck," Danny yanked his daughter back. "Go over and take care of that car for me, will ya?"

Becky tossed her head. "Why me?" she said hotly. "So you can play with this mutant here?"

"Becky!" Danny pulled her out of hearing range of Spike. "Becky, listen. I know it's hard. But with this guy on the team, we've got an actual shot at this thing. So, just give me a minute so I can get him used to the idea of playing with a girl, okay?"

Becky bit her lip. "You don't think I can take him do you, Daddy?" Danny didn't answer. Becky looked over at Junior. He looked back at her sympathetically. But the rest of the team were staring down at their sneakers.

Becky's eyes flashed. "I think this is a buncha junk!" She stormed off the field.

Spike grinned, but the other kids looked miserable.

"Okay," Danny said weakly. "Let's get back to business, okay?" The members of the team nodded and slowly jogged out on to the field. Danny called the play. Junior shot a pass to Hanon, who dropped it immediately. Zolteck, who was supposed to be the head lineman, lost all sense of direction and ran the wrong way — right into Spike. And in the middle of all this chaos, little Timmy pulled out his cap gun and started firing.

Danny tried to put the best face on things. "Hey," he said. "Now we're starting to look like a team."

Spike rolled his eyes. "You call this a team? It's more like a telethon. Hey . . . you . . . " he pointed at Junior. " Mr. Pretty Boy. When you handoff, you give it to Spike. Boom! No one else. And you, fat lineman . . . " Spike jabbed a finger in Zolteck's direction.

Zolteck rolled his eyes backward. "You rang, Master?" he said in his best Lurch imitation.

"From now on, get your jelly rolls out of Spike's way, unless you want Spike's cleat marks up your fat back!"

"Uh . . . everyone got that?" asked Danny.

The kids nodded.

"Okay, Nubie, what are we running next?"

"Let's see," Nubie whipped open his PowerBook computer and typed on the keyboard. "Oh, it's a great one. The Pitch and Stitch, a new invention of mine."

Spike shook his head. "Ditch the Pitch and Stitch!"

"Ditch the Pitch and Stitch!" Danny echoed.

Nubie's shoulders slumped.

"The only play you gotta know," Spike boomed, "is put the ball here." He gestured at his huge open hand.

"You heard him," said Danny. "The only play you gotta know is . . . give the ball to Spike!"

The kids exchanged troubled glances. What was going on? Was this going to be all they did as a team from now on? Give the ball to the Spike monster?

"He talks like a caveman!" muttered Zolteck.

"He is a caveman!" declared Hanon.

"You heard what Spike said, kids." Danny didn't even seem to notice their discomfort. "Now, let's play ball!"

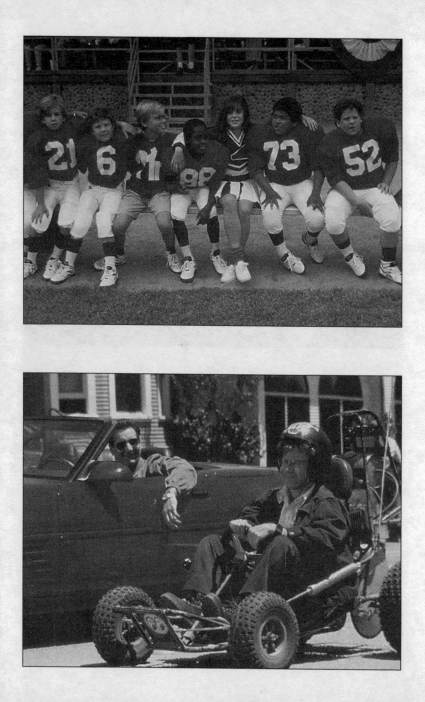

CHAPTER TEN

BECKY SAT IN THE CORNER BOOTH
of the Coffee Cup Cafe picking gloomily at a plate of French fries.
"It's no use. I'm not hungry."

"The Icebox not hungry? Alert the media!" Kevin slid into the
booth across from her. Becky sighed and looked out the window.

"Still mad at me for not picking you, huh?"

"No."

"Yeah, I guess you've got your own team now."

"No." Becky turned to look at her uncle. "It's Spike's team.
Dad's got this real big crush on him."

"Ah, Beck. Don't be too hard on the old man. Can't be too
easy having me as a brother . . . or you as a daughter."

"Ha, ha. Very funny, Uncle Kevin."

"It's true, Becky. People like me and you can be pretty
stubborn. If we don't get our way, watch out!"

"You mean that when you were playing football, you wanted to
kill your coach, too?"

"Hey, Beck." Kevin snitched a French fry. "You can't fault a
guy for trying to win."

"He doesn't want to win," Becky said. "He just wants to show
everyone he's not scared of you."

"How about you? What do you want?"

Becky rested her chin in her hand. "I don't know. I *thought* I
wanted to win, but now there's all this other stuff."

Was Becky really saying she was miserable playing for the
Little Giants? There was a sudden gleam in Kevin's eye. If Danny
lost Becky, he didn't have a hope of winning. All Kevin had to do
was help Becky make up her mind.

"What sort of stuff?" he asked, trying to sound like a concerned uncle. Becky looked at him. Kevin felt a twinge of guilt. But then he reminded himself: All's fair in football and war.

"Not football stuff," Becky sighed.

Kevin flashed his killer grin. "Glad to hear it. Do me a favor and tell Priscilla you're starting to think of other things besides football. She really looks up to you, Beck. All she ever asks about is when she can start playing on my team."

"Really? What did you tell her?"

"I told her exactly what you're finding out now. Girls don't have a future in football. And instead of trying to be like her cousin, she should try to be more like her big sister."

Becky sighed again. "Debbie likes Junior, doesn't she?" she said.

"Does Tinkerbell like Peter Pan? Does Minnie like Mickey?"

"She's gonna get him. I know it," Becky said in a dejected voice.

Kevin put on a concerned expression again. "Hey, Beck, nothing's for sure. Debbie would kill me if she knew I was telling you this, but if you want a boy, you gotta figure out how boys think. If the boy is a quarterback, he's probably looking for a cute girl, not a teammate."

Becky bit her lip. "I don't know about being a cute girl, but I'm good at sports."

"Of course you are. You're an O'Shea, aren't you?" Kevin winked at her. "But take it from your old uncle. You've got a lot more going for you than just football."

Becky eyed him doubtfully. "Really?"

"Really."

"Do you think I'm pretty, Uncle Kev?"

Kevin shook his head. "Nope." As Becky's face fell, Kevin went on, "I think you're *beautiful!*"

Becky's face lit up. "Thanks, Uncle Kev," she whispered. "I gotta go. See ya!" She got up and skipped out the door.

• • • • •

"Okay, let's run the play again," Danny said. Becky watched from the sideline.

Spike clutched the ball under his arm and rocketed down the field. Within moments, he had mowed down the entire defensive line.

"Give me a hand, Tad," Zolteck moaned. "I feel like every bone in my body has been brutally crushed."

"Me, too," Tad muttered. "This is getting really . . . old."

"Yeah," Zolteck pulled out a bag of Cheetohs. "At least when Murphy beats us up, it's more personal!"

Suddenly an angry booming voice shouted from the end of the field: "Where in tarnation is Danny O'Shea?"

The color drained from Danny's face as Mike Hammersmith came storming out on to the field. "So," the giant man fumed. "You're the Heisman Trophy winner, huh?"

"I never *actually* said I was Kevin O'Shea," Danny sputtered. "I only said I was Coach O'Shea!"

"Yeah, right, bozo!" Mr. Hammersmith turned to Spike. "Get in the car, son," he thundered. "You're a Cowboy now!"

Spike threw up his arms. "Thank you! Thank you, football god!" He tossed the football at Danny and ran after his father.

The members of the team saw that Kevin's Corvette was pulled up on the side of the road. Danny saw it, too. "Mr. Hammersmith — wait!" he called.

The big man turned and glared at him. "What for?" he sneered. "Why you puny little . . . ." He took a giant step toward Danny. Danny took an equally giant step back.

"Now, is there anything else you want to say?"

Danny looked like he was about to faint. "Uh . . . no, sir."

Mr. Hammersmith jumped into the Corvette. Kevin poked his head out the window. "See you, baby bro'," he cried cheerfully.

"Great," said Zolteck. "Now *those* guys have Spike."

"And we got nothing," cried little Jake Berman.

"We got *us*," put in Tad hopefully.

"Yeah, and we *stink*," Hanon declared. "Get a life, Tad."

"Just 'cause you can't catch, 'Hot Hands.'"

"At least he can walk, tinman," said Zolteck bitterly.

"Hey, hey, guys," Danny protested. "C'mon, that's enough."

"Coach is right," said Junior. "Break it up."

Zolteck rolled his eyes heavenward. "Oh, shut up, Junior. You're so good it makes us sick!"

"Hey, you don't want me to play? No problemo." Junior turned and strode off the field.

Becky looked at Zolteck. "Nice work, moron. If it wasn't for him, we wouldn't even have a team."

"Hey," Hanon piped up, "if it wasn't for *him*, maybe you'd stop *drooling* and play a little football, Icebox!"

Becky shoved her helmet onto her head. "That's it," she shouted. "I'm outta here."

"Becky, wait!" Danny called. He looked around at what was left of his team. "Okay guys," he said softly. "Practice is over."

"Why can't we just be *friends?*" Tad wailed, tears spurting into his eyes. "Why can't we all just *play* together?"

"Quit bawlin' you big baby," said Zolteck.

Tad turned on him furiously. "I can cry if I want!" he yelled. "It's a free country. I can even do this." He kicked Zolteck as hard as he could in the shins and dashed off.

"Yoooowwww!" Zolteck doubled over.

"Hey," cried Marcus, impressed. "Nice kick!"

● ● ● ● ●

Tad stumbled down the street. "What's the use?" he lamented. "What the guys said back there is true. I am a dipstick. I'm never gonna get to play."

"Hey, squirt! Got a sec?"

Tad lifted his head. Pulled over against the curb, right next to him, was a monster bus. Tad peered up at the tinted windows. A bunch of guys were sitting inside. Big guys. Very big guys. In fact, they were kind of monster-sized, too.

"Over here, squirt!"

A familiar-looking man poked his head out of the front window of the bus. He walked over to him.

"Yeah? What d'ya want?"

The man smiled. "Well, you see, me and my boys got a

banquet to get to in Canton. Y'know, at the Football Hall of Fame? But we must have taken a wrong turn somewhere . . . ."

Tad was no longer listening. He was too busy staring. Now he knew who the man was, but it was impossible! What was John Madden, legendary coach of the L.A. Raiders, doing here? In Urbania?

"Hey," Tad squeaked, "are you *really* John Madden?"

"Yup." The man nodded. "That's me, son. Like I was saying, me and my boys must've taken a wrong turn somewhere. Now look here —" John Madden pulled out a map and held it out of the window. "We started *here*, right?" He marked a big black "X" on the map with a felt-tip pen. "Then we rolled out along the I-70 East, picked up the 104 *here* — Bam! We cut back to 4-9er, and tried a short cut through Routes 10, 12, 48 — hut!"

Tad, grinned to himself. So this was how legendary football coaches talked — like the whole world was a football field!

John Madden stared at him. "You follow, squirt?"

"Yes, sir."

"Anyway, as I was saying, we've got to hit Canton, and hit it *hard* — Wham! But I don't know where the heck I am. So can you help us, squirt?" John Madden stared at Tad.

Tad studied the map. "Sure, no problem," he said coolly. "Take this street two lights up, and make a left. Then go right at the next light; that's Lancaster. Just ignore the sleeping cow in the intersection, that's Sherman. Belongs to Old Man Whittacker. Go left onto Conrad until you hit the interstate."

Madden folded up the map. "Thanks, son. I owe you one. Remember the name: John Madden. If you ever need a favor, you call me."

He rolled up the window.

"John Madden," Tad said in awe. Then it hit him. John Madden! The bus released its brakes and started to roll forward. "Hey!" he screamed. "Mr. Madden! Wait!"

The window rolled back down as the bus reapplied its brakes.

"What is it, son?"

"Maybe there is *one* thing you can do for me . . . ."

CHAPTER ELEVEN

TAD TIPTOED UP TO THE OPEN DOOR of the go-cart shed and peered inside. The guys were all there, slumped around the card table. He had never seen a bunch of kids look more depressed. "Uh, guys?"

Zolteck looked up, his face orange with crumbs. "Now what?" he demanded.

Tad stepped aside, revealing several thousand pounds of professional football players behind him. The kids gawked as Emmitt Smith, Bruce Smith, Steve Entmann, Alvin Harper, Tim Brown, and John Madden piled into the room.

Tad grinned. "Let's play some ball."

• • • • •

Out on the field, a huge fist with a picture of a Jolly Roger tattooed across the knuckles slammed down against the turf. A pudgy, smaller fist slammed down nervously across from it. Steve Entmann and Zolteck were facing off.

"Okay," said Steve Entmann, gazing at Zolteck from beneath his fearsome eyebrows. "Take a shot and block me!"

Zolteck shook his head firmly. "Uh-uh."

Entmann chuckled. "Come on," he drawled.

Zolteck eyed him. "No way!"

"You can do it!" Entmann insisted. "Go for it." The other members of the team burst out cheering. "Come on, Zolteck," they hollered. "Do what the man says."

Zolteck took a deep breath, puffing out his cheeks. "Okay," he grunted.

He smiled a tiny smile and rose to his feet. Bending his head down, he rushed forward like a round cannon ball. Bam! Entmann toppled backwards onto the grass.

Zolteck let out an astonished breath. "Oof!" Then he grinned. "I did it!"

The huge player winked at him. "That's right, kid. Now just remember: Football is eighty percent mental and forty percent physical."

Zolteck's grin widened. "Right, Mr. Entmann." Then he paused, a puzzled look on his face. "What?!"

Emmitt Smith sat on a bale of hay with all the Little Giants around him. He eyed them, one by one. "Do you guys feel like winners?" he asked them seriously.

The kids fidgeted awkwardly. "Yeah," they mumbled.

Emmitt Smith gave them a look. "Wait a minute. Do you guys feel like winners?"

"Yeah." This time the 'yeah' was a little stronger.

"You think you can win."

"Yeah!" The kids were starting to get into it.

A gigantic smile spread over Emmitt Smith's giant face. "Good," he said. " 'Cause that's where it all starts. Believing in yourself. Believing that you can win!"

"Yeah!" the kids shouted it this time.

On the other side of the field, Junior rocketed a pass to Hanon. Hanon leaped up, touched it, and then watched it roll out of his fingers again. He stared at his hands. "Thanks, fellas." He looked up and saw Tim Brown coming toward him.

"Y'know, Hanon," Brown said, "I was always fast, like you. But I couldn't catch. Then my older brother told me, 'Don't think of it like a football, think of it like the softest thing you've ever touched — something you can really get a grip on.'"

"Like what?"

Tim Brown pulled out a roll of toilet paper from his jacket pocket. "Something squeezably soft," he chuckled. The big man backed away, drew his arm back, and passed the roll through the air to Hanon. It kited across the sky. Hanon reached for it, caught it, and *held* on. Hanon looked down at his hands, and a huge smile burst over his face. "I did it! I did it!"

Tim Brown shrugged. "I told you you could."

• • • • •

Inside the shed, Nubie was scribbling on the chalkboard like a madman. John Madden watched intently.

"See," Nubie explained, "he pivots, fakes left, and chucks the big bomb downfield to our — hopefully — wide-open tailback! I call it the Annexation of Puerto Rico." He frowned. "Except we don't have a tailback," he added glumly.

Madden squinted at the squiggly lines on the board. "Not bad," he said, impressed.

Nubie turned to look at him. "Really?" he asked eagerly. "I kinda stole it from you. Raiders/Packers 1966. Third quarter, fourth down —"

"Touchdown!" the two of them shouted the word together.

Madden laughed. "*You* are a genius, kid. Hand me that chalk, would ya? Listen, what if you tried this instead . . . ."

Madden began scribbling all over the chalkboard as wildly as Nubie had been. Nubie started to smile. "That's beyond genius, Mr. Madden," he breathed. "It could work! And with no tailback. Let's call it the Annexation of Alaska!"

• • • • •

Bruce Smith paced up and down in front of Zolteck, Tad, Timmy, Marcus, Jake, and Johnny holding a football. "You know what this is called?" he asked.

The kids shook their heads.

Bruce Smith popped the football between his hands. Pow! Up rose a geyser of air and dust. The kids' mouths fell open.

"Intimidation," the huge man chuckled.

The kids exchanged glances. They were intimidated all right.

"Now tomorrow," Bruce Smith went on, "during the game, you don't want to be intimated. Now let's see your game faces."

The boys tried to put on mean faces. But their expressions looked more terrified than tough.

Bruce Smith looked at them and shook his head. "Nah, he snarled. "Those aren't game faces. This is a game face." He twisted his features into a fearsome scowl.

"Aghh!" The kids backed away.

"And if that doesn't work," Smith added, "try this." He reached into his pocket and pulled out a huge Alka Seltzer tablet. "You know what this called?"

Zolteck took a guess. "Relief?"

"Uh-uh." Newton popped the tablet into his mouth. "Intimidation." He smiled. His mouth foamed like a rabid dog's.

Danny sat in the office of the gas station, trying to keep his mind from the game. The Little Giants were going to lose big-time, and it was all his fault. If only he hadn't gotten carried away with Spike, Danny thought, everything might be very different. Just then Danny heard a whistle blow. Toot! Toot!

Danny glanced out the window. "Hey," he rose to his feet. The practice field was crowded with kids — kids and . . . .

"Football players?" Danny exclaimed. He ran outside and tore out on to the football field. The huge men playing with the kids looked like FAMOUS football players; and the man blowing the coach's whistle was a dead ringer for John Madden, one of the greatest pro football coaches of all time.

By the time Danny reached the man who looked like John Madden, he was completely out of breath. "Hey," he wheezed. "I know this is gonna sound nuts, but are you —"

The man didn't give him time to finish. "John Madden. Sure am." He stretched out his hand. "You the coach?"

"Yeah. Danny O'Shea."

Madden grinned and glanced up at Urbania's Water Tower. "Kevin O'Shea's brother?!" he asked excitedly.

"Yeah."

Madden paused. "Never did like that guy." He turned to Danny. "Boy, you got it licked here. Great bunch of kids, dirt field, *mud*, homemade goal post! This is where football should be played. Not in some glass dome with fake grass and sky boxes."

Danny smiled. "Thanks . . . Coach."

"No, thank *you*." Madden smiled back. "Now me and the boys better get a move on if we're gonna make Canton. See ya." He headed toward the bus. The other players had already started to board.

"Hey, Coach!" Danny called. Madden stopped. "We've got kind of a big game tomorrow. Got any advice?"

Madden thought a moment. "Good luck!"

Danny's face fell. "That's *it*?"

Madden shrugged. "Listen," he said, "there's no big secret to winning football. Just do what these guys do," he jerked his thumb in the direction of the gleaming silver bus. "Go out there and give it your best."

Madden started walking again, then stopped once more.

"Bottom line, Danny?" he said. "I took a bunch of guys nobody wanted and won a Super Bowl with 'em. You guys are a *football team*! That's just like family. You boys *stick together*. You're gonna be fine."

Danny looked at the kids. Their faces were glowing. They were soaking up Madden's every word, wanting to believe it. Danny wanted to believe it, too. "Yeah. I guess we are a team," he said softly. "Thanks, Coach." Madden waved and got onto the bus. The engine started and the bus slowly pulled away.

"Tell me I'm not dreaming," said Hanon.

"You're not dreaming," replied Zolteck.

"How do you know?"

"'Cause I pinched myself — sixty-three times," he groaned.

CHAPTER TWELVE

KEVIN RAISED THE FOOTBALL above his head and gave the boys gathered around him an intense look. The Cowboys' last practice session before the big game had just ended. Kevin was about to give the team his pre-game pep talk. He pointed at the ball.

"People, this ain't just a football!" Kevin declared in a voice trembling with emotion. "It's your hopes, your dreams, your ambitions. It's your life — your soul on a roll!

"Out on that field tomorrow, it's DO OR DIE! WIN OR CRY! And boys," Kevin pinned them with his eyes. "We're here to win."

Cheers resounded across the field as the Cowboys leaped to their feet. "Right on, Coach!" they shouted. "You said it!"

Kevin held up his hand and everyone fell silent. "Now," he said, his voice soft and low. "Go home tonight, brush your little teeth, wash your little faces, and go to sleep, dreaming the sweet dreams of football glory!"

The eyes of the boys listening misted over. Kevin smiled.

It was a perfect moment. Then, the perfect moment was abruptly destroyed by a sound — the whine of a go-cart engine!

As everyone stared aghast, Becky's go-cart came whizzing out on to the field. Becky was driving and Junior was beside her. They looped around the field, screaming as loudly as they could: "LITTLE GIANTS!"

Pandemonium broke out on the field as the Cowboys took off after Becky and Junior. Kevin tooted on his whistle like a lunatic. "Okay, guys! Get back here! Now!"

The go-cart circled the field and drove off. The Cowboys ran back to their coach, red-faced and out of breath.

Kevin put down his whistle. "Now listen, guys," he said grimly, "never mind what they say 'cause tomorrow we're gonna crush those Little Giants to smithereens!"

"Yeahhh!" The Cowboys' shouts shook the entire stadium.

•　•　•　•　•

Becky sat on the overturned boat at the edge of Urbania Lake. She snuck a peek at Junior who was sitting beside her. Nearby, a beach blanket was spread out on the grass. A teenage couple was sitting on it, kissing passionately.

"Ugh," said Junior. "That's really disgusting. It looks like they're trying to swallow each other's heads or something."

"Yeah," agreed Becky. "They're doing it all wrong. You're supposed to be real dramatic about it and romantic and stuff. Kind of like Kevin Costner in *Robin Hood*."

Junior stared at her. "What are you talking about?"

"I'm just saying how you're supposed to kiss, that's all. You're supposed to do it more like this." Becky wildly kissed her own hand to demonstrate.

Junior shook his head. "No, no. In the movies they always do that chicken-peckin', mouth half-open kind of stuff."

"Really?" Becky asked. "You mean like my friend Trina's older sister and her boyfriend?"

"What?!" Junior was confused.

"Well, Trina says her older sister and her boyfriend always French kiss. That means they use their tongues . . . I guess."

Junior stared at her in horror. "Why?!"

Becky shrugged. "I don't know. Anyhow," she said in a low voice, "you know what the only problem with kissing your own hand is?"

"No, what?"

"It doesn't kiss back," she whispered.

Junior suddenly looked very nervous. "Hey, Becky, why are we talking about this? I hate kissing."

"Hey, its not that bad." Becky looked over at him. "Anyway,

we're gonna have to learn how to do it sooner or later. I mean, if you want to be a grownup and have kids and stuff . . . ."

"So I'll never grow up." Junior replied.

"Yeah, but . . . what if you were forced to learn how to kiss? Don't you think it would be kinda good to learn with a real close friend . . . for scientific reasons?"

Junior inched down to the edge of the boat. "No way. If I had to — and I mean if I absolutely had no choice no matter what — I think I'd want to do it with . . . ." he broke off, his face red.

"Let me guess. Debbie?"

"I don't know." Junior fidgeted awkwardly.

"Well, if not her, definitely another cheerleader-type, right?"

Junior looked away. "Maybe . . . ." he mumbled.

Becky gazed out at the lake again. "I bet if I was more like that then you'd want to learn with me."

"Hey, but you're not," said Junior. "You're different, Beck. You're the Icebox. You're my pal. Plus, you're the first girl I've ever met that could probably beat up my dad."

"Gee, thanks."

"I mean it, Icebox. Look, I'll see ya later, okay?" Junior waved and walked off.

Becky stayed where she was. After a while, she lifted her head. "The Icebox, huh?" she said. "Well, not any more."

• • • • •

Kevin had only been home a few moments when the doorbell rang. He scowled and threw open the door. But when he saw who was there, his scowl vanished. It was Becky, and he could tell she was upset. "Hey, Beck," he said, making his face serious. "What's up?"

Becky looked away. "Nothing much, Uncle Kevin," she mumbled. "Is Aunt Karen here? I need to talk to her."

"Girl stuff, huh?" Kevin said. "Come on in," he smiled broadly. "I'll go get her for you right away!"

• • • • •

Danny stood staring at himself in the mirror in the front hall. He screwed up his face. "Oh, no you won't," he snarled. "This team has come too far to be shot down by a lousy call."

Danny grinned at his reflection. "Not bad. But maybe not quite coach-like enough." He stuck a baseball cap on his head backwards and pretended to kick dirt at an umpire.

"What d'ya mean you'll throw me out?" he protested. "I'll throw you out. I'll throw your mother out. I don't care if this is the Super Bowl; I'll do whatever I want!"

Suddenly, Danny saw that Becky was standing behind him. "Hey, where've you been? I didn't even hear you come in." He noticed she was carrying a large flat cardboard box under her arm. "So do I look authentic or what?"

"Uh . . . you look great, Dad." She started for the stairs.

Danny pulled her back. "Hey, wait up. You can't just sneak outta here without telling your old coach what's in that box."

Becky looked down. "It's nothing."

"It can't be nothing. Let me guess. A victory cake in honor of tomorrow's big win?" He reached for the box.

Becky pulled away. "It's not a cake, Daddy."

Danny grinned. "Okay," he said. "My little fullback wants to surprise me! That's okay."

Becky glared at him. "Little fullback?" she said furiously. "That's all I am to you, isn't it, Dad? Your little fullback, your ticket to beating Uncle Kevin and winning the game!" She burst into tears.

Danny gazed at her in shock. "Becky, what's wrong?"

"Everything's wrong," Becky sobbed. "Do you know what Mom used to call me? Her little princess. Every night when she tucked me in, she said, 'Goodnight little princess.'"

Danny blinked. "How can you remember that?" he said in a hoarse voice. "You were so —"

"Small?" Becky's voice was muffled. "Well, I do remember, okay? Mom might have let me play football, but she would never have called me her little fullback!"

"Becky," Danny swallowed hard. "Your mother isn't here. She left us. She quit."

"No, she never quit, she just found a better team. I'm the one that's quitting."

"What are you talking about?"

"I'm not playing tomorrow, Daddy."

"What do you mean you're not playing? You said this game was the most important thing in your whole life —"

"No, Dad," Becky shot back, "that's the problem. I think it's the most important thing in your whole life."

She ran past him, and the big cardboard box tumbled out of her hands and burst open. A brand-new cheerleader's outfit fell onto the floor. Becky disappeared up the stairs. Danny bent over and carefully picked up the bright new sweater and skirt.

"Where've I been?" he said aloud.

CHAPTER THIRTEEN

IT WAS THE MORNING OF THE BIG game. The Little Giants were in their dressing room waiting for Danny. Outside, the streets of Urbania were hung with banners announcing the big event. The Little Giants were nervous and keyed up, but trying not to show it.

"I prayed to the football god all night long!" announced Jake Berman as he entered the locker room.

"So? Did he send you a sign?" asked Zolteck.

Jake shook his head. "I don't know, but my night light burned out," he answered hopefully.

"Sounds like a sign to me," Hanon frowned, and gazed down at his hands. "I practiced catching passes with my Dad 'til way past my bedtime."

"Did you catch any?" demanded Johnny Vanero.

Hanon gloomily shook his head, but then he brightened. "I think I will today, though," he said. "A guy's luck has gotta change sometime, right?"

The kids stood on tiptoe and stared through the window at the rapidly filling stands. Zolteck spotted his parents in the front row, sharing a box of chocolate-covered doughnuts. Bonk! Zolteck grinned as Tad Simpson's father, lugging a huge video camera, stumbled over a couple of Cowboy parents and sent them sprawling. "Way to go, Mr. Simpson," he yelled.

He turned to Johnny Vanero, who was studying the crowd silently. Where's your dad? I thought he was definitely coming today?"

Johnny shrugged. "Last-minute business trip."

"Too bad," said Tad. "'Cause this game is gonna be —"

"A real shoot-out," finished Timmy Moore, who had just come into the locker room, trailing a giant cannon behind him. The others ogled him. "Hey, man, what's that?" Hanon asked.

"It's my dad's cannon. He said I could fire it if we scored any touchdowns," Timmy replied.

"Hey, awesome!" said Zolteck.

The Little Giants were starting to feel pumped up and ready. But where was Danny?

• • • • •

In the locker room next door, Kevin was trying to call his team together for a moment of prayer. He wasn't having any luck, because the Cowboys were even more pumped up than the Little Giants. At last, Kevin bellowed, "SHUT UP!"

He gestured at the white-haired priest beside him. "Father Kelly has to catch the 11:30 bus back to Hamilton to bless some baby, so stop your yapping and kneel down for heaven's sake!"

"Yes, Coach O'Shea, sir." The boys knelt.

"Go ahead, Father."

Father Kelly's eyes twinkled. "Very good, boys. Now, as we are about to embark on this journey of athletic competition, we pause to reflect that it is not whether we win or lose, but . . . ."

That was as far as Father Kelly got; Kevin suddenly interrupted him. "Yo, Padre, could we have a word? Now about that winning and losing stuff . . . ." Kevin whispered something in Father Kelly's ear. The priest's eyes bulged. "Excuse my language, Father," Kevin said, "but do you see my point?"

The priest gulped and nodded."Well, now," he began again.

A loud pounding sound drowned out Father Kelly's words. "What in the world —" Kevin exploded. Then a muffled shout rose through the wall. "GIANTS! GIANTS! GIANTS!" Next door the Giants were pounding on their lockers and shouting with all their might.

With an angry roar, the Cowboys rushed over and started pounding on their lockers. "COWBOYS! COWBOYS! COWBOYS!" they shrieked.

• • • • •

On the other side of the wall, the Little Giants were going nuts. Timmy Moore was firing his cap gun, and Zolteck was swinging from the door of his locker like an oversized Tarzan. "Hey, Briggs, you big snot ball," he yelled as he swung. "I'm gonna eat you for lunch!"

Just then Danny walked in, carrying a large cardboard box. "Guys!" He set the box down onto the floor. "Hold on!"

Tad, who had climbed up on a bench, turned to wave at him. "One sec, Coach!" Tad put his mouth to the air vent. "Paging Spike the no-necked moron!" he hollered. "The Icebox is about to defrost you for good!"

Danny cleared his throat. "Fellas, stop, please —"

Nubie wriggled his eyebrows at him. "Relax, Coach. We're unstoppable."

The door to the locker room suddenly swung open, and everyone turned to see who it was. For a moment, there was stunned silence. Then Hanon shook his head. "Tell me I'm dreaming," he moaned.

"You're not dreaming," said Zolteck. "It's the Icebox."

"Was the Icebox, you mean," muttered Johnny Vanero.

Becky O'Shea was standing before them dressed in a cheerleader's uniform. She was even holding pompoms. Her hair was pinned on top of her head and on her lips she was wearing . . . .

"Lipgloss!" Junior looked like he was about to faint.

Becky smiled at him and glanced around at her old teammates. "Hi, guys. I just came by to wish you luck. Have a great game. I'll be rooting for you." She turned and ran out. The door slowly clicked shut behind her.

The team stared at it, motionless.

"Guys," Danny said, helplessly, "we're gonna be fine."

They all turned toward him in disbelief.

"Fine?!" shouted Marcus. "Without Becky we're gonna be cream of wheat."

"Yeah," moaned Tad. "Icebox was my shield. Without her, Spike's gonna rip my face off and wear it for Halloween."

"Look, nobody's gonna get hurt out there," Danny said.

"Well," said Nubie. "I must say, she looked cute."

"A fox," Hanon agreed mournfully.

"Who cares?" burst out Zolteck in a panic. "She's not gonna be playing with us. I'm outta here. I'm leaving the country. I'm going to New Mexico!"

"Good idea!" The entire team headed for the door.

"Guys," Danny called after them, "wait a second. There's something I want to show you." He ripped open the box in front of him and pulled out a brand-new football jersey with the words "Little Giants" written across it. The members of the team stared at their new uniforms.

"Death shrouds," said Tad.

"Come on, I even got your names on the back."

"So the guys at the morgue can identify the bodies," declared Jake Berman.

Nubie ran his hands through his hair. "Sorry, Coach, but like Zolteck said, we're outta here."

Once again the team moved toward the door.

Danny rushed in front of them. "Guys," he pleaded. "You have to trust me. There's nothing to be afraid of."

"Not for you," retorted Marcus. "You're not the one who's gonna lose 78 to 0 in front of the whole town."

"Is that what you're afraid of?" Danny asked. "Losing?"

No one answered. They didn't have to. The answer was written on their faces.

"Well, let me tell you guys something." For once Danny's voice was strong and commanding. "You've already won. Just by suiting up here today, you've showed those Cowboys — heck, you've showed this whole town what courage is all about."

"We won?" Tad looked confused.

"And if you don't believe me, I can prove it." Danny reached into his pocket and pulled out a dog-eared paperback. "This is my favorite book. It's called *Guys Who Didn't Get Picked But Refused to Quit*. Wait 'til you see what good company you're in."

Turning his back on them, Danny shielded the cover of the book as he hastily rifled through the pages.

"Let's start with a little kid who was so small . . . ." Danny turned around to face them again, "they used to laugh when he showed up to play ball. But he said, 'I'll work hard and grow eleven inches and show those jerks that there's nothing I can't do if I put my mind to it.' And three N.B.A. championships later, he became a living legend!"

Marcus's jaw dropped. "Michael Jordan was short?"

"Technically he was a midget!" Danny replied.

"And how about a young man named Ken Griffey Junior," he went on, "who weighed two hundred pounds in the fifth grade and was never allowed to swing the bat!"

"Hey!" Zolteck's eyes flew open. "Ken Griffey Junior was fat?"

Danny nodded. "He still goes to Weight Watchers twice a week, because he wants to show those jerks who wouldn't let him play that he *belongs* on the field. And that calling him 'bubble butt' was a big mistake!"

Zolteck's eyes almost popped out of his head. "They called Ken Griffey Junior bubble butt?!"

"And even though Michael Jordan was a midget, he still tried to play?" broke in Marcus.

"Uh-huh," said Danny. "The harder they laughed, the earlier he laced his shoes."

The guys all looked at one another.

"I say we play," piped up Tad, his voice shaking. "We play for all the guys who got laughed at — like Michael Jordan!"

"Yeah!" cried Zolteck. "Let's do it for bubble butt!"

"Hooorah!" the team all screamed.

Danny smiled proudly. "Now you're talking. You can do it! You can blaze! You can blast! You can play! You can—"

"Fly!" burst out little Timmy Moore. The others stared at him. His voice sounded funny. Then they realized why. Timmy was singing. "Fly, you can fly, you can fly."

> "When there's a smile in your heart,
> There's no better time to start . . . .
> It's a very simple plan . . . ."

"Hey, has he lost it or what?" whispered Hanon.

"Nah. He's just singing," Zolteck replied. "You know, the theme song to 'Peter Pan'?" Hanon shook his head. "It's great," Zolteck said earnestly, and he put his hand on his heart and began to sing, too:

> "You can do what birdies can —
> At least it's worth a try . . .
> You can fly, you can fly!!!"

On the other side of the wall, Kevin and Father Kelly started as the singsong voices of Zolteck and Little Timmy came warbling through the air vent: "You can fly! You can fly!"

A look of disgust came over Kevin's face. "I don't believe this," he fumed. "This is supposed to be a football game, not a Broadway musical!" He glared at his team. "Okay, which one of you is humming along?" No one moved.

CHAPTER FOURTEEN

THE STANDS WERE PACKED.
The local sports announcer, Clip Carson, sat in the press box, holding a microphone. At last, Carson shouted into his microphone: "Hello everybody. Here come the Cowboys coached by the colossal Kevin O'Shea, All-American Heisman Trophy winner!"

To a drumroll by the elementary school band, Kevin O'Shea and his Cowboys burst through a homemade banner held by up two cheerleaders. The other cheerleaders made a tunnel of pompoms. The crowd roared as the boys dashed through it.

With much less enthusiasm, Carson went on. "And here comes the other team, the Little Giants, coached by first time coach and non-athlete Danny O'Shea!"

Two cheerleaders held up a much smaller, shabbier banner. The Little Giants, dressed in their new uniforms, headed toward it. But as they reached it, Jake Berman's helmet slipped down over his eyes and he stumbled and fell. The rest of the team tripped over him, landing in a big messy heap at the foot of the banner. Jake peered up at Danny. "I told you I couldn't see with this thing on!" he said crossly. Danny slowly shook his head.

•　•　•　•　•

Danny and Kevin stood at mid-field next to Mayor Kelly and the referee. Mayor Kelly was holding a microphone and talking to the crowd. The game was about to begin. All that remained was the coin toss to decide who was going to kick off.

"Welcome to the park, folks," Mayor Kelly boomed. "Today

we're going to see a contest we'll never forget. Kevin's Peewee Cowboys are gonna flex their mini-muscles against Danny's Little Giants to see who's gonna take on Sutterville."

Mayor Kelly reached into his pocket and pulled out a quarter. "Okay, Kevin, you call it," he said and tossed the coin.

Suddenly, Danny reached out and grabbed it in mid-air. "Excuse me, but why does he get to call it?"

Kevin turned on him. "What does it matter? Either you'll kick off and we'll ram it down your throat. Or we'll kick off, take it from you, and *then* ram it down your throat."

Mayor Kelly's microphone picked up every word Kevin said and broadcasted them throughout the stadium. The crowd was leaning forward, hanging on to every word.

"Whoa! Coach fight," said one woman.

"Yeah!" said the man next to her. "This is better than pro wrestling!"

"Well, I think it's disgusting," snapped another woman, holding her hands over her child's ears. "Such language!"

Out on the field, Danny was getting mad. "Oh, yeah, Kevin?" he shouted. "Who do you think you are? You've been bossing me around since we were kids, and I'm sick of it!"

"This is football, Danny," Kevin shouted back. "You don't ask for things, you take them!"

"Just like you took my ticket to that World Series game with Dad?" Danny demanded.

"Come on, guys," Mayor Kelly pleaded. "Stop this. You're brothers —"

"Not by choice!" Danny fumed.

"Back off, Danny," snapped Kevin. "I will not take this trash from a man who invested every dime he had into a run-down wreck of a gas station!"

"Run-down wreck!" Danny yelped indignantly. "That gas station has been servicing this town for forty years. It's a landmark!"

"It should be a landfill!"

Danny's chin jutted out. "You know what your problem is, Kevin? You don't know anything about heart —about loyalty! I'd put that gutsy little station up against any business in this town."

Kevin started to walk away, then turned back. "Oh, really?" he said in an icy voice. "Well, that's fine with me!"

"Good, then its fine with me, too!" Danny stormed, then he paused. "Uh, Kevin, what exactly are we talking about?"

Kevin smiled. "Your gas station against my dealership, little bro'. Whoever wins the game wins it *all*!"

Danny turned white as a ghost. Then he slowly nodded. "You're on!" he said.

"Great. I'll even let you call it. Go ahead, Danny."

Danny took a deep breath. "Heads."

"Open your hand," Kevin said. He did. Kevin smiled.

"Tails it is!" shouted the referee.

"Danny," Kevin said, "this is going to be the longest day of your life!"

"We'll see about that," Danny retorted. He turned and started over to his team. But when he saw the ragged bunch of kids hunched awkwardly on the sideline, his heart skipped a beat. "What am I doing?" he muttered to himself in sheer terror.

● ● ● ● ●

They were seconds from kickoff. Both teams were gearing themselves up. Kevin's team was shouting, "Cowboys! Cowboys! Cowboys take all!" Danny's team was shouting, too. "Little Giants, Little Giants, help us, God, please!"

"Hey, folks," Clip Carson shouted. "Are you ready for some football?! The Giants will be kicking off. They're defending the western goal. My right, your left as you listen."

"Yeeeaaaahhhh!" the crowd exploded.

Marcus took his place, ready to kick the ball. Johnny Vanero was holding it for him. Just as Marcus was about to kick, Nubie dashed out on to the field. "Now listen, Marcus," he babbled nervously, "hang time is key, so try and kick the ball high toward the northeast sidelines, somewhere between a 30- and 40- degree angle."

Marcus nodded. "No problemo."

"Good . . . I hope." Nubie ran off the field. The ref blew his whistle. Marcus stepped back, then ran up and kicked as hard as he could. The only problem was he didn't kick the ball. He kicked Johnny Vanero.

Johnny's eyes bulged out of his head. He toppled forward, screaming in agony. "Mar-cus! You kicked me right in the . . . ."

Marcus looked down at him. "I know! I'm sorry, Johnny. Honest! But where's the ball?" The two of them looked. The ball had rolled six inches, and the Cowboys were all over it.

"So much for the first play," groaned Nubie from the sideline. Danny blew his whistle, calling the team together.

"Okay," he said. "Rocky start — kinda — but hey, that doesn't mean a thing. Now, here's what you have to remember, guys. Defense is the key to this whole game . . . ."

● ● ● ● ●

When the Little Giants came back onto the field, the Cowboys were already in position. The looks on their faces sent shivers of terror through the row of Little Giants who were supposed to block them. Not only were the Cowboys bigger, faster, stronger, and better-coordinated than they were, but they seemed ecstatic to have a chance to beat up their opponents. Even Zolteck felt about three feet high and three inches wide as he crouched over the line, nose to nose with Sean Murphy.

"Hey, Zolteck!" Murphy growled.

"What?!" Zolteck tried to sound tough, but instead he sounded what he was — terrified.

Murphy grinned. "Get ready, dogbreath, 'cause when I get through with you, your head is gonna be sticking up through your legs, and your arms are gonna be twisted around your feet!"

"Uh," Zolteck turned to Tad. "Is that physically possible?"

"Hike!" called the quarterback. Zolteck started to move, but Murphy rolled right over him like a speeding Sherman tank. Zolteck had just enough time to see Spike breaking out into the open field with half the Giants chasing him, when his legs were pushed out from under him, and his face was shoved into the dirt. He grimaced and shut his eyes. When he opened them again, Tad was leaning over him.

Tad looked down at him in amazement. "Yeah, Zolteck," he said slowly. "I guess it is physically possible."

Zolteck just groaned.

• • • • •

The Little Giants were gathered in a huddle at the new line of scrimmage. Their faces were long and gloomy. "Hey," said Junior. "Cheer up. There's still time to turn this thing around."

"Yeah, right," the others said.

"If a good guy on a white horse shows up," piped up Timmy Moore, "we just might have a chance. But otherwise . . . ." He drew his finger across his throat.

Little Timmy was right. During the next play, Spike rushed for twenty yards, knocking Zolteck, Tad, Little Timmy, Jake, Johnny, and Junior into the dirt. In fact, Spike could have gone all the way on that one, except he accidentally went out of bounds. On the play after that, Spike rushed for thirty yards, crashing the Little Giants' defense as if they were a bunch of paper dolls. This time the only thing that stopped him was his own shoelaces.

On the play after that, Spike roared down the middle, knocking Zolteck and Tad as flat as pancakes. Soon the only standing between him and the goal line was Timmy Moore. Little Timmy watched in horror as Spike advanced closer and closer. He knew he should turn and run for his life, but he couldn't move! Spike had all the room in the world to score a touchdown without even coming close to him. But the big ugly grin on Spike's face told little Timmy that he was planning to slam right into him.

"Help! Help!" he shouted, but it was too late. Bam! Spike sent him flying. Crunch! Little Timmy landed deep in the end zone next to Spike and the football. "Touchdown!" the referee roared. Spike raced back to his teammates to celebrate. Little Timmy cautiously wriggled his arms and legs to see if anything was broken. The other Little Giants came running over to him.

"Hey, Timmy! Are you okay?" Hanon asked.

Little Timmy lifted his head. "Did I pass the spelling test, Mrs. Greely?" he asked groggily.

Zolteck's eyes popped open. "Mrs. Greely?" he said. "Wow!" Spike knocked him back to second grade."

"Great," muttered Hanon.

Danny shouted angrily at the referee from the sideline, while Becky and the other cheerleaders looked on. "Come on, ref," he yelped. "This isn't American Gladiators! That was a cheap shot. You'd better put a leash on Spike."

"Like I told you," the referee replied. "No penalty."

"No penalty!" Nubie was outraged. "Come on, ref. Don't you care who wins?"

Meanwhile, out on the field, the Cowboys were kicking for the extra point. They got it. The scoreboard lit up as Carson announced gleefully, "Cowboys, 7; Little Giants, 0."

The Cowboys whooped and butted their heads together. The Little Giants watched in stunned silence.

Priscilla raised her pompoms and bravely started a Little Giant cheer:

> "Chickens cluck, pigs waller . . . .
> All for the Giants
> Stand up and holler!"

But no one did. Becky stared down the crowd. "She said to stand up and holler!" she shouted. The crowd looked at her, then stood up and started cheering.

The two teams took to the field again. This time the Giants were on offense.

"Remember, guys!" Danny shouted after them. "The key to this game is offense."

"Huddle," called Junior. The Little Giants huddled.

Junior turned to Hanon. "Now, Hanon, I want you to run a bear trap curl. And try to catch it, okay?"

Hanon nodded. "It's a sure thing," he said positively. While the others raced out onto the field, Hanon reached into his pocket and pulled out a "Sure Stick." He quickly coated both his hands with it and ran out to the field.

Junior called the signals. Hanon raced out to the far sideline. Suddenly, he realized that both of his hands were together. His mouth open, Hanon stared down at himself in horror.

"Uh-oh," he said to himself.

"Hike!" Junior shouted. Hanon ran desperately down the middle of the field, struggling to free his hands. But they were glued tight. Junior whipped back for the pass. Hanon tried to signal him to stop, but Junior throw the ball straight towards him. Hanon jerked at his hands frantically, but it was no good. The ball dropped down and bounced off his shoulder.

The fans in the stands started laughing. So did the Cowboys. "Nice catch, 'Hot Hands,'" taunted Spike.

Hanon's face fell.

●　●　●　●　●

Spike was running along the sideline past the cheerleaders, when he and Becky locked eyes. "Howdy, Icechest — I mean, Icebox," Spike leered. Becky took a step toward him, but Debbie pulled her back.

"Becky!" she hissed.

Becky spun around to face the crowd again, a huge fake smile plastered on her face. Waving her pompoms, she jumped high into the air, leading the others in a new chant.

> *Let's all roll, let's all rock,*
> *Let's all get the pit-bull blocked!"*

"That's better," Debbie whispered. "Now, remember, Beck, cheerleaders don't get into fights, okay?"

"Yeah, right," Becky mumbled. Debbie started to breath a sigh of relief until she noticed that Becky still had her eyes fixed on Spike, and if looks could kill, Spike would be dead.

• • • • •

The game rolled on. With each play, the Cowboys advanced further and gained more confidence, while the Little Giants were ground deeper and deeper into the dirt. Even Junior, the team's best player, couldn't seem to get anything started. On the sixth play, he took the snap and tried to run around the left side. Giants fans cheered, but before he'd gone five yards, six Cowboys brought him down with an earth-shaking thud!

On the sidelines, Becky was still cheering her heart out. As the next play began, she leaped to her feet and shouted:

> "Don't be frightened, don't have fears!
> Junior, look, the middle's clear!"

Junior grinned at her as he took another snap and tried to run with it. But Spike soon brought him down in yet another bone-crushing tackle.

"No first down," Carson declared from the press box. "The Giants will have to kick again."

Looking sad and defeated, the Little Giants lined up for the punt. Spike glared at Jake, who was across from him.

"Hey, squirt, Spike's gonna rip your head off!"

Jake hastily tucked his head down under his shoulder pads. As Marcus came up for the punt, Spike lunged forward and knocked off Jake's helmet. Then he and the other Cowboys rushed in to block Marcus's kick. The ball came down, bounced off Jake's helmet and landed neatly in the end zone, where Spike triumphantly dived on it.

The scoreboard lit up again. It now read: "Cowboys - 14, Little Giants - 0."

• • • • •

The Cowboys were gathered on the sideline, about to head back out onto the field. "All right gentlemen," Kevin said happily. "We've dug the hole, now let's go shovel the dirt over the rotting cadaver!"

His team looked up at him in confusion.

"The rotting what?" asked Briggs.

"The rotting candy bar, stupid," Murphy shot back.

"Huh?" said the others.

"Never mind," bellowed Kevin. "Just score more points. Score more points. Now!"

"Oh, yeah, right!"

The Cowboys and the Giants were lined up at the 50 yard line. Briggs lowered his head. "Down! Set! Go!" he shouted. Junior moved after Briggs, who faked a pass to Murphy, then pitched the ball to Spike. As Junior sacked Briggs, Spike took off down the field. The Spike Monster soon mowed down Hanon, Marcus, Johnny, and Zolteck. Only Tad was still standing. Summoning all his courage, Tad seized Spike by the jersey and tugged as hard as he could. But Spike didn't even slow down. Instead, the jersey began to stretch and stretch as Tad was dragged remorselessly down the field.

From the stands, Giant fans look on in dismay. But at the Giant bench, Danny was going crazy.

"Thatta boy, Tad!" he hollered. Keep going! You've got daylight! Go for it!"

Nubie looked up at Danny in shock. "Uh . . . coach . . . what are you talking about? Tad doesn't have daylight. He doesn't have anything."

"Oh." Danny frowned. "He doesn't?"

Meanwhile Tad was being bounced down the length of the field. "Help! Heeelp!" he shrieked.

"Let go!" his teammates shouted from the sidelines.

"I can't! Tad shouted back. "He's going too fast. If I let go, I'll go ballistic."

"Well, do something!" Zolteck yelled at him.

Tad just moaned. "I should have gone to camp! I should have taken up golf! What am I doing here?"

As Spike ran across the goal line and stopped, Tad finally let go of Spike's jersey. Kerblang! Tad flew up in the air, and came crashing down with a sickening thud. "Another Cowboy touchdown!" Clip Carson shouted happily into the microphone.

Zolteck fell backward on to the turf. "Oh, brother." The scoreboard lit up once again: "Cowboys - 21, Little Giants - 0." Just then a gun sounded.

"What's that?" shouted little Timmy. "Are they gonna start shooting at us now?!" He reached for his cap guns, forgetting he wasn't wearing them.

"Calm down," Hanon told him wearily. "It just means the first half of the game is over."

"Oh," little Timmy looked around. "That's not good is it?"

The others shook their heads.

"Not when you're losing as big as we are," said Nubie.

CHAPTER FIFTEEN

BEATEN, BRUISED, AND DEPRESSED,
the Giants limped toward the tunnel to the locker room. As they
stumbled across the field, the Cowboys taunted them from the
sidelines.

"See ya soon, beanbags!" hooted Murphy.

"Yeah!" Spike grinned. "Have a nice half-time, girls!"

"Guys, don't listen to them," Danny begged. "We're still in this
game!"

"Yeah, right," grunted Zolteck. "Hey, Marcus, look at my back.
Is that my spine sticking out through my uniform?"

Marcus looked. "I don't know. It's kind of hard to tell."

"Hanon, go call 911," moaned Tad.

Hanon stared down at his hands, sadly. "I can't, man," he said.
"My fingers are stuck together."

The team lurched into the tunnel. Danny was about to go after
them, when Kevin came sauntering over. "Great first half, Danny."
He grinned. "A real nail-biter."

"Hey, it's not over," Danny replied stubbornly.

"Look," Kevin sighed, "this has gone far enough. Maybe you
should call it off. Put your boys on the injured list."

Danny tried to hang tough. "The injured list?"

"Yeah," replied Kevin. "The injured list." He started jogging
down the tunnel. "Oh, and don't worry, Danny," he called over his
shoulder, "there's always gonna be a job for you at the full service
pumps!"

A crushed-looking Danny stared after him. "Oh, God," he
groaned, "tell me *please*. How could I have been so *stupid?*"

• • • • •

When Danny walked in, the kids had already taken off their new jerseys. They were splayed out on the benches, their shoulders slumped, their faces grimy and bruised. Danny stared at them, and he took a deep breath.

"Okay, guys," he said, trying to sound upbeat and positive. "We've still got a shot at this. We'll do one or two things a little differently, and we're back in there . . . ."

His players just sighed. Then Tad pulled a book out from behind his back. It was the paperback Danny had used during his pre-game speech, only instead of being called *Guys Who Didn't Get Picked But Refused to Quit*, it was a Sunoco Gas Station Service Manual from 1965.

"Michael Jordan was a midget, huh?" demanded Marcus.

"Yeah, and Ken Griffey Junior was fat!" put in Zolteck.

"Okay," said Danny quietly, "I lied. But I lied for a good reason. I lied because you all worked so hard, and I wanted you to get in the game. I'm sorry."

"Sorry doesn't cut it, Mr. O'Shea," Zolteck said. He handed Danny his jersey. "What about the second half?"

"Just say we're hurt or we all got stomachaches," said Tad.

"Yeah," Hanon nodded energetically.

"NO!" Danny's voice rang out through the room.

"What do you mean, NO?!" protested Zolteck. "If we go out there, we're dead and you know it!"

"Guys," Danny cleared his throat, "we're a team and teams don't quit. They work together. I forgot that when Spike was playing with us, and I'm sorry I did. I owe you an apology. And, there's something else you should know. When I was ten years old, I put myself on the injured list, and I never got off."

"Why?" Tad asked.

Danny shrugged. "I didn't get picked to play a few times, so I started hiding under the bleachers."

"That's where we belong — under the bleachers," said Marcus.

"No, that's not true!" Danny took a step toward them. "I know you guys are as good as those Cowboys," he said, with feeling. "I know because I was as good as Kevin O'Shea."

Zolteck burst out laughing. After a moment, the others joined in. "Give us a break, Coach," Zolteck sputtered. "We know you. You could've never beat Kevin O'Shea at anything."

"No, you're wrong." Danny's eyes clouded over. "When we were kids, Kevin and I would always race our bikes down Cherry Hill. We'd race every day after school, but I could never win. Ever. But then this one time . . . this one time, I beat him!"

Jake Berman raised his eyebrows. "You beat Kevin down Cherry Hill?"

"He ate my dust! It happened!"

"Big deal," Johnny Vanero said. "One time."

"Yeah," said Tad. "But you know," he paused, "one time at Randy Cooper's swim party I did a back flip off the high dive, and my big brother chickened out."

"Roger chickened out?" cried Marcus. "But he's a marine!"

No one was laughing anymore.

"Hey, that's nothing," put in Zolteck. "One time I beat both of my brothers in the Spring Carnival cow pattie toss."

"You beat Matt and Brad in the turd toss?!" said Tad.

"Yup!" Zolteck smiled proudly. "They were so burned up, they wouldn't talk to me for a *week*!"

"Once I went fishing with my whole family," piped up Jake Berman suddenly, "and I was the only one who didn't throw up!"

"Whoa!" everyone shouted. "Way to go, Jake!"

"See," Danny nodded at them, "there are times when everything goes our way, and we can actually win!"

"Yeah, Coach," Marcus shook his head, "but that still doesn't make us good football players."

"Whoever said you had to be good to play football?" Danny demanded. "You play because you want to, because it's fun. Remember our practices?"

Smiles appeared on a few faces. "Yeah!"

Danny pressed his point home. "That's why you play! Not just to be good, but because you wanna run around and make believe you're Joe Montana throwing touchdown passes to Jerry Rice."

All the members of the team were smiling now.

"Maybe those guys next door," Danny gestured at the Cowboy locker room, "are better. Maybe 99 times out of a hundred they'll beat us. But even if that's true that still leaves . . . ."

Tad leaped to his feet. "One time . . . ."

"One time . . . ." echoed Zolteck, rising beside him.

The others rose to their feet, too.

"One time!" they all chanted.

"You've got it," said Danny. "One time . . . ."

•   •   •   •   •

When Danny came down the tunnel with the Little Giants behind him, Kevin was waiting for him at the entrance.

"It's okay, Danny," Kevin said as he came up. "I already told the mayor you're forfeiting."

"You did?!"

"Yeah. I could see it in your eyes. You were ready to quit."

"Well, you'd better turn right around and tell the mayor you were wrong," Danny said. "'Cause we're not quitting."

"I admire your spirit, Danny, but you keep forgetting one thing." Kevin pointed up at the water tower with the words "Football's Kevin O'Shea!" painted across it. "This is my field."

"Yeah," replied Danny. "But we get the ball."

•   •   •   •   •

Both teams were in position for the kickoff. "Okay folks," trumpeted Carson from the press box. "The second half of the Peewee showdown is on its way!"

Beaurigard kicked the ball for the Cowboys. It soared up, then flew down into the waiting arms of Junior Floyd. Junior started running. Ahead of him, Zolteck, Hanon, and Tad rushed at the line of Cowboy defenders. Whap! Both sides crushed into each other. The ref blew his whistle.

To the amazement of the crowd, the Cowboys were slow to get back up on their feet again. Meanwhile, the Little Giants were going crazy — headbutting and trading high-fives across the field. Maybe they hadn't made any progress — yet — but at least they'd stood up to the Cowboy line.

• • • • •

The Little Giants gathered for their first huddle. They were a different team from the one that had blundered out on the field forty-five minutes earlier. They were really pumped up now, and although they didn't know what this would mean — or if they could do anything about it — they could feel the difference.

Junior Floyd grinned at his teammates. "Men, time to put our game faces on. Here's Nubie to explain the play." His hair sticking up like a mad scientist's, Nubie whispered his instructions. "And remember what Steve Entmann told you," he said to Zolteck as he headed back to the sidelines.

"What?!" Zolteck said in confusion, then snapped his fingers. "Oh, yeah, right!" he smiled broadly.

The Cowboys looked on nervously. Junior was under center with the rest of the team gathered around him. The Little Giants glared at the Cowboys across the line of scrimmage.

"Hey," Tad sneered at Patterson, his bright red hair showing like flames beneath his helmet. "When I'm finished with you, they're gonna have to ship you home in a body bag."

"Wha!" Patterson stared at him in shock.

"Yeah," Hanon growled at Briggs. "Prepare to eat grass!"

Meanwhile Zolteck leaned toward Murphy. "Hey, pig breath," he said, preparing to snap the ball. "You're in big trouble!"

"How come?" Murphy responded coolly.

"Because football is 80 percent mental and 40 percent physical," Zolteck grunted.

"Say what?"

"Hike!" Junior shouted. Zolteck snapped the ball. As Junior grabbed it, he charged ahead, flattening Murphy beneath his immense bulk. Beside him, Tad smashed into Patterson as hard as he could. The bigger boy looked down at him in shock. "OOOF!" he said, before he dropped to the turf.

Meanwhile, Junior faked a pitch to Johnny Vanero and then dashed through a small hole in the line. He started running, but didn't get too far before Spike viciously tackled him.

"Ouch!" cried all of the Giants, but then they saw where Junior had fallen. Hanon let out a whoop. "Hey, guys . . . look!"

Tad blinked. "I don't believe it. We've gained a yard!"

"Wait," exclaimed Zolteck. "That's no yard. That's a yard and a half."

Junior was on his feet again. "Hey!" he called to the others. "We can beat these guys."

"Folks," announced Carson from the press box, "it looks like second and nine and —" Carson stopped in surprise. "No, I take that back. It's eight and a half! No, that's not wax in your ear — you heard the word 'gain' with Giants on offense."

The crowd went crazy. Flashbulbs flashed, banners waved, and Becky led the cheerleaders in a rousing Giant cheer. From the sideline, Danny looked on in shock. "Allright! We got a yard!"

At the opposite side of the field, Kevin turned to Mr. Hammersmith. "All this fuss over one lousy yard!" he scoffed.

"Hike!" Junior called out on the field.

The Giants rushed forward. They were on a drive now. Bam! Down fell Beaurigard, Murphy, and Briggs. Junior swerved around to the left side, dodging through the Cowboy defense.

"He's going for it, folks," Carson hollered as Spike came around to bring Junior down yet again. When the dust cleared, however, the crowd saw that Junior had gained five yards!

"That makes it third and four," announced Carson.

On the next play, Junior made a pitch to Johnny, who threw a screen pass back to Junior, who rushed down the field, gaining thirty yards. As the Little Giants exploded into cheers, Carson said into the microphone, "First down, Giants!"

The crowd led out a thunderous roar.

"First down," muttered Kevin. He turned to Mr. Hammersmith. "Doesn't mean a thing."

Out on the field, Junior took the snap. Once again, he ran around the left side. Only this time, he handed off to player 99 — Tad Simpson — on the reverse. Tad tucked the ball under his arm and headed down the field. Meanwhile, Spike ran up and pulverized Junior, not realizing until after the tackle that Junior didn't have the ball.

Carson was shouting so loud he was losing his voice. "And the reverse works," he cried breathlessly. "Player 99 has got daylight with only two defenders to beat!"

Tad turned and saw the two huge Cowboys close on his heels. "Yiiiikes! I'm dead! I'm dead!" he shrieked.

"Get out of bounds!" Danny shouted at him.

"Yeah! Run for your LIFE!" chimed in Zolteck.

Tad zoomed toward the sideline. Just as he was about to step out of bounds, however, he slammed on his brakes and ducked. The two Cowboys who were right behind him were going to fast to stop in time. Instead, they charged past Tad and smashed into a Gatorade cooler set up by the stands.

Tad stared at the drenched Cowboys, unable to believe his luck. "I'm alive! I'm alive!" he marveled.

"Hey, Tad!" Danny's voice was as piercing as a whistle.

"Yeah, Coach?"

"Run!"

Tad looked down. His toes were right against the sideline. He was still in bounds! Then he turned and saw that the entire Cowboy team was thundering after him.

"I'm dead! I'm dead," Tad babbled.

He turned and raced down the sideline. The Cowboys pounded after him. Tad went faster, his head down, the football clenched tightly under his arm. "Heeeeelp!" he hollered. Just then he realized that he had crossed into the end zone. A look of pure astonishment came over his face.

"And it's a touchdown for the Giants!" squawked Carson. "What a play! What an incredible play by number 99 and Junior Floyd! It looks like Mr. Momentum may be changing his address."

Now the crowd was out of control. Cowboy fans were booing and Giant fans were going crazy with happiness. Danny was the only one who wasn't cheering. He was too stunned by what he had just seen.

"We did it," he repeated over and over. "We did it. We scored a touchdown!" He looked down to see little Timmy Moore with a sly grin on his face, rolling out his father's cannon.

"Can I, Coach?"

Danny nodded. "Sure thing, Timmy. Fire one!"

The cannon fired. Around the stadium people dived under their seats and then cheered all the louder. To the joy of some and the dismay of others, the cannon blast had knocked the head off the statue of colossal Kevin O'Shea that stood in the stadium entrance. Kevin's face went red with rage. "My statue," he fumed. "They did that on purpose."

Danny chuckled and turned around to wave at Patty Floyd who was in the stands right behind him. Patty was on her feet, pumping her fist in the air. She looked . . . . "Gorgeous!" Danny whispered as the ref blew his whistle for the extra point kick.

Looking small but fierce, Marcus dashed toward the ball. Johnny, who was holding the ball for him, winced. "Hey, Marcus," he hissed. "Just don't kick it — you know, where you kicked it last time."

"I won't," Marcus promised. He lifted his foot. Johnny paled, and a number of people in the stands ducked. Bam! The ball soared straight up and then dived down again, just barely bouncing over the goal post.

"Extra point good!" proclaimed the referee.

Marcus threw up his arms and jumped up as high in the air as he could. "I did it!" he crowed. "I did it!"

The scoreboard lit up. To the wonder of everyone present, it now read: "Cowboys - 21, Giants - 7."

Danny's eyes glistened with pride. He looked over at his team. "I told you so, guys," he mouthed at them. "We're back in the game!"

CHAPTER SIXTEEN

KEVIN SAT IN THE CENTER OF THE
Cowboys' huddle. "Guys," he said. "I want 42 points up on that board or no Pizza Hut! Understood?" His players gulped and nodded.

As they started out to the field, Mr. Hammersmith pulled Spike back. "All right, Spike," he whispered, "We're not taking any chances. Either take Junior Floyd out of this game, or I'll rent your darn bed out to a boarder. You got that, son?"

The ref blew his whistle, and the Giants kicked off. Murphy took the kick and ran out to the middle of the field. Junior was waiting there for him. Pow! Murphy was flattened. As Junior fell on top of him, the referee whistled the play dead. But from the left side, Spike kept charging toward them. With a grin on his face, Spike pounced on Junior with all of his force. "Hey, no fair!" Junior protested as Spike's helmet slammed into his middle like a speeding hammer. Junior gasped.

"Junior!" Patty shrieked from the stands in horror.

Danny leaped to his feet, furious. "Hey, what's going on here?" he demanded. "The play was over!"

He rushed out on to the field. Junior was lying on his back groaning. Spike was standing over him. "Geez," he said. "Guess I just didn't hear the whistle."

The referee and several parents rushed out on to the field, followed by a doctor. "Stand back, boys," the doctor commanded. "Give him some air." Junior moaned.

Watching from the sideline, Kevin winced as he saw Junior carried off of the field. It was hard to see a good player get really hurt unfairly — even if he was playing for the other side.

"Great move, huh?" said Mr. Hammersmith.

Kevin's mouth became a thin line. "No," he replied. Reaching out, he grabbed Mr. Hammersmith by the collar. "If your little monster does somethin' like that again, you're both out of here!" he growled.

"But . . . ." Mr. Hammersmith stuttered, pulling away, "I thought you wanted to win."

"Not if it means pulling tricks like that," Kevin responded. To his surprise, he realized he meant it.

● ● ● ● ●

Out on the field Danny and Patty were helping to carry Junior off the field in a stretcher. He was white as a sheet and obviously in pain. Becky ran forward, her lip trembling. Suddenly, Spike shoved past her.

"What's the matter, Icebox?" he sneered. "Upset 'cause your little boyfriend got a tummy ache?"

Carson's voice crackled over the loudspeakers. "And it looks like trouble for the Giants. Their comeback won't go much further with Junior Floyd out of the game . . . ."

Becky glared at Spike. Pushing her way through a cluster of cheerleaders, she strode over to a pile of pompoms. Reaching under them, she lifted up a shiny, brand-new Giants helmet!

● ● ● ● ●

Across the field, Kevin was giving his team another last-minute pep talk. "We've just got to get our momentum back. Remember, you've gotta follow through out there . . . ."

Kevin realized no one was listening. Instead, the Cowboys were staring at the field with stunned expressions on their faces.

"Holy cow!" said Murphy.

"Is that . . . ." Patterson's voice trailed off.

Now Kevin saw what they were staring at. It was Becky. She had on a Giants helmet and shoulder-pads. She was charging out on to the field, and the fans were on their feet, cheering.

"What the blazes is that cheerleader doing with a helmet?" Mr. Hammersmith demanded.

"That's no cheerleader!" Kevin replied, with a worried frown. "That's my niece, Becky, and she's mad!"

• • • • •

Becky started out on to the field. Danny ran up to her. "Becky, are you sure you want to do this?"

"Uh-huh. And Dad? Call me Icebox, okay?"

Becky glanced anxiously back at Junior. He was sitting on the bench, wincing in pain. But he tried to smile when he spotted her. "Kill 'em, Icebox," he said.

"I will. And Junior? Call me Becky, will you?"

She trotted out to the mid-field. Suddenly, Spike stepped out in front of her.

"Hold it, Icebox. Maybe you oughta think this over. You step on my field and you're mine."

Becky sneered at him. "Oh yeah, Spike. Well a woman can only dream." She shoved him aside and jogged over to her teammates to join the huddle.

"Now listen, guys. I just have one thing to say: I'm sorry I let you down in the first half."

Her team smiled at her. "You didn't let us down," chirped Jake Berman. "You cheered great!"

"Yeah," Becky rolled her eyes. "I helped carry Junior's stretcher, too. But that's not enough. *This* is where I belong. Here with my *team*. Now, are you guys with me?"

"Yeah! You bet, Icebox."

"Okay, let's go!" Becky let out a war whoop.

The Giants were on the defense once again. Briggs was the quarterback for the Cowboys. It was plain that he was going to hand off to Spike. The Little Giants quickly decided on their strategy. As the play began, Becky positioned herself across from Spike and waited for the snap.

"Hike!" Briggs shouted nervously. Snap! Briggs grabbed the

ball and handed off to Spike. Spike started his drive. But the Little Giants, led by Becky, crashed through the Cowboy blockers like a bunch of mini-Godzillas. Soon, they caught up with Spike. He tried to break away, but Becky shoved him into the dirt. "Agggh!" Spike groaned as the ball popped out of his hands and rolled away. Hanon jumped on it, and the referee blew his whistle loudly.

"Hanon covers it tighter than the lid on a pickle jar!" Carson announced. "Giants' ball."

On the Cowboy sideline Kevin frowned while Butz wrung his hands together like an anxious grandmother.

But on the Giants' sideline all was smiles. "It's working, Coach!" Nubie declared. "We're acting like a team!"

"Yes," said Danny. "We . . . ." he broke off as he spotted a familiar-looking man in a suit climbing up into the stands.

"Who *is* that?" he wondered aloud. "Could it be? It is!" He lifted his head. "Hey Zolteck, come here. Tell Becky the next play's gotta be Chicken Little flea-flicker on two."

"Sure, Coach." Zolteck ran over to Becky and whispered in her ear.

"Are you sure?" she mouthed.

Danny nodded.

The Giants got into a huddle. "All right," said Becky calling the play. "Chicken Little flea-flicker on two. That's a pitch to Johnny."

Johnny Vanero looked up, startled. "A pitch to Johnny?! But you can't pitch to Johnny. I'm Johnny!"

"That's right," Becky said calmly. "Zolteck, he's gonna need a hole."

"Can we talk about this?" Johnny wailed. But Becky and the others were already heading out to the line of scrimmage.

Zolteck was standing in front of Patterson and Murphy. Suddenly, he clutched his stomach. "Maybe you guys could help me," he gasped. "I'm trying to remember what I had for lunch."

"How could we help?" Murphy wanted to know.

"Well, I feel like I'm about to barf," Zolteck said, "and maybe you could take a look and . . . ."

Murphy and Patterson took a quick step backward.

"Oh, no, Zolteck's gonna barf!"

More Cowboys backed away from the line. Kevin gazed at the field in confusion as a large gap formed in the Cowboys defense.

"Hike!" Becky yelled. Zolteck snapped the ball to Becky, who whirled around and pitched it Johnny. Johnny's eyes widened in panic. "Now what?" he demanded.

Becky pointed at the end zone. "Run toward him."

Johnny followed her finger. There in the end zone stood a man in a suit waving at him. Johnny's mouth fell open. "Dad?" he said.

"Johnny!"

"Daaad!" Johnny took off, just as the Cowboy defense was about to come down on him. He zipped and twisted down the field, racing around players, leaping over players, and ducking *under* players. The Cowboy defense gazed after him in shock. Johnny Vanero was unstoppable.

"Dad!" Johnny made forty yards, and holding the football over his head, he crossed the goal line and dashed into his father's arms. His father lifted him up and twirled him around.

"That's my boy!" Mr. Vanero was glowing with pride.

"Another Giant touchdown!" Carson shouted as little Timmy Moore fired his cannon from the sideline.

Kevin looked on in disbelief. "A family reunion?!" he shouted across the field at his brother. "This isn't Donahue, Danny-boy. It's football, for pete's sake!"

The scoreboard lit up again. Now it read: "Cowboys - 21, Giants - 14."

• • • • •

The teams took the field again. The Giants were still charged up from their latest touchdown. But the Cowboys were charged up, too, and ready to do whatever needed to be done.

It was the Giants' kickoff. Spike crouched down at the mid-field line. "Hike!" shouted Briggs. Spike thundered forward. But before he could even make five yards, Becky, in pure Icebox mode, dragged him down in a punishing tackle. The next play was the same. Smoke was practically coming out of Spike's ears.

"Spike is death," he intoned. "Spike don't get stopped by no girl!" The ball was snapped again. Spike raged forward. This time though, it wasn't Becky who stopped him, but Timmy Moore. The last thing Timmy wanted to do was get in Spike's way. But in his eagerness to stay out of trouble, Timmy ran way over to the sidelines. When Spike ran that way to dodge Zolteck, Timmy found himself right in front of him. "Help!" he hollered. But little Timmy was so small, Spike didn't even see him until he tripped over him. Ooof! Spike landed on his back, and the ball rolled out of his hands.

"Play is dead," announced the referee. "Giants' ball."

On the next play, Zolteck snapped the ball and Becky grabbed it. She started to race down the field, but Spike drove her out of bounds and tackled her at the Cowboy bench.

"No first down," Carson announced. "The ball goes back to Kevin's Cowboys."

Once again, both teams were at the 50-yard line. The Little Giants had just brought Spike down to the ground for the second down. As the players got to their feet, Murphy leered down at Jake Berman. "What's the matter, four-eyes?" he demanded, poking Jake in the goggles. "You want your mommy?" Jake glared at him furiously. "Don't be talking about my mama," he squealed angrily. Murphy laughed and walked away.

Both teams lined up again. Briggs took the snap and handed off to Murphy. Murphy shoved his way through the Giants' line of defense.

"He can see daylight!" Carson yelled.

But just then Murphy was flattened by none other than Jake Berman. Murphy blinked at him in awe. "You!" he sputtered. Jake shrugged modestly. Just then Cheryl Berman's voice came thundering down from the stands. "That's right, Jakester!" she snarled. "Rip their filthy ears off!"

Jake smiled sweetly and waved. "Yeah, Ma!"

Murphy moaned. "I think I'm going to be sick."

• • • • •

Becky was fired up now. She leaned into the huddle. "Okay, it's still their ball," she said. "But we're rabid dogs, and they won't get past us!" She threw back her head and howled like a wolf. Beside her Nubie was busy handing out pieces of Alka Seltzer. "Remember, guys," he said, "intimidation!" The Little Giants ran out to the line.

The Cowboys took one look at them and turned green.

"They're a bunch of animals!" whimpered Patterson.

"Yeah . . . it's gross!" wailed Briggs.

Briggs handed the ball to Spike as if it were a hot potato and quickly stepped aside. The Little Giants rushed forward and trampled Spike to the ground.

"Giants' ball!" Carson announced.

• • • • •

Becky called the play. "Oscar Meyer weiner, sheena queena, ballerina. One, two — break!"

"Hike!" Becky shouted. She faded back to pass, but before she could get the ball in the air, Spike clawed his way up Murphy's back. Then, using him as a launching pad, he sailed through the air and landed on top of her. She hadn't even made a single yard.

"It's still 21-14, folks," declared Carson, "and there's only 3:48 on the clock!" The Little Giants have fought hard, but it looks like their hopes of a Pee-Wee victory are fading fast."

The Cowboys grinned. They were getting their confidence back. Becky called another play. But Spike sacked her before she could advance a single yard.

The Little Giants grimaced at each other. Danny called a time out. "Now, listen, guys," he said. "You can't give up now. Zolteck, you've got to look for that opening. If they blitz, you've got to pick it up!"

"Yeah, Coach, but . . . ."

"Call the next play!"

"But what should it be?" asked Becky.

"Silver streak to Hanon," the words popped out of Tad's mouth, and everyone looked at him in surprise.

"Okay," said Danny. "Silver streak it is."

Hanon looked scared. "But what if I mess up again?" he asked.

Danny held up his hand. In it was a roll of toilet paper. "You won't," he said. "Just think Charmin. Two-ply. Squeezably soft!"

• • • • •

The Little Giants were ready to go. "Okay, guys," said Becky. "One, two." Becky took the snap and faded back to pass.

"Blitz!" Danny hollered from the sideline.

Briggs was about to sack Becky, but at that very moment, Zolteck dropped back and delivered a staggering block. Briggs fell over. Becky, seizing her chance, let the ball fly.

It soared through the air like a bird . . . or a plane. Hanon streaked down the field, his eyes fixed on the spiraling football. Then, as he gazed up at it, it seemed to turn into a roll of Charmin right before his very eyes!

"Charmin. Nice and soft," Hanon told himself. "Squeezably soft." He grabbed the ball and stumbled over the end zone.

The ref blew his whistle. "Touchdown!" he roared.

Hanon grinned as his father and mother dashed down from the stands to hug him. He felt like a hero.

"I caught it! I caught it!"

On the Cowboy sideline, Kevin slammed down his clipboard.

Mr. Hammersmith grabbed Spike as he came off the field. "Losing will not be tolerated, Spike!"

Bing! The scoreboard lit up. The game was tied at 21-21 with 1 minute, 45 seconds to go.

"One more touchdown," Kevin told his players. "One more touchdown is all we need. Now, get out there and do it!"

CHAPTER SEVENTEEN

BECKY LOOKED AROUND THE HUDDLE.
She was so exhausted, she couldn't see straight. She could tell the rest of the team felt the same way. "And it's their ball," sighed Timmy Moore.

"Yeah," said Becky. "There's only one thing to do."

"What? Go to sleep?" said Zolteck.

"No! We're gonna have to stop Spike!"

"We can't. He's too strong!"

"Yes we can. We can do it . . . together!" Becky's eyes were shining.

• • • • •

"Hike!" Murphy took the hand-off and gave it to Spike. The monster-sized kid blasted through the line. All the Giants tried desperately to hang on to him. But Spike just kept lurching along. He dragged them for ten yards before little Jake finally managed to land him.

"First down, Cowboys!" the dreaded words blasted through the loudspeakers. The Little Giants hung their heads. "Don't give up!" Becky encouraged them. "We can do it!" But the next three plays went exactly the same. Spike advanced down the field, advancing the Cowboy's chances of victory with each step. There were only 36 seconds left in the game, and Spike was drawing ever closer to the end zone.

"Well, these Little Giants have sure put up a fight," exclaimed Clip Carson. "But it doesn't look like they can keep this up much longer . . . ."

"You can say that again," mumbled Zolteck. "I've got aching muscles where I didn't even know there *were* muscles!"

"I know," sighed Becky, "but we just have to keep going . . . somehow!"

The Little Giants limped up to the line of scrimmage. Spike took the ball and came bulldozing towards them. Down went Zolteck. Down went Marcus. Down went Tad. "Get up!" Becky shouted "Get up!" They did and managed to catch up with Spike as he crossed the five-yard line. Using every last ounce of their strength, they brought the mountainous Spike down at the one-yard line. On the sideline, Kevin and the other Cowboys were cheering wildly.

Across the field, Danny hung his head. "So close and yet so far," he said to Nubie, who stood gloomily at his side. Just then, someone tapped him on the shoulder. He turned to see Patty Floyd smiling at him.

"Hey, Patty . . . ."

"Danny," Patty said urgently. "Do you remember that championship game with Sutterville when we were in high school — the one where Kevin scored the winning touchdown?"

The corners of Danny's mouth turned up. "Do I ever!" He rushed out on to the field. "Time out!" he yelled.

Danny's players peered up at him. "I just want you all to know," Danny began, "that no matter what happens, you guys really are Giants . . . ."

Becky sighed. "Dad, would you just get off the field? We have to stop them and —"

"I know, I know. There's just one more thing. Back when we were kids and the game was on the line, Kevin liked to run a halfback sweep to the left."

Becky lifted her head. "You sure about that?"

"Uh-huh."

"Okay, guys," Becky shouted. "Huddle!"

• • • • •

Both teams were lined up at the one-yard line. Becky stood across from Spike, whose whole body was straining toward the end zone. The Giants crouched forward, waiting for the ball to be snapped. Suddenly, Becky stood up. "Shift," she hollered.

To the Cowboys' shock, the entire Giant defense suddenly moved to the left side of the ball.

On the sideline, Kevin slammed his clipboard across Butz's head. "They know the play!" he screamed.

"Two, twenty-four . . . ." Briggs was calling it. Snap! Briggs caught it, turned and handed off to Spike.

Spike took two steps forward, and instead of following the play and going left, he turned and headed right!

"After him!" Becky shouted in desperation. But no one heard her. It was just her and Spike. She was the only one between Spike and touchdown glory. Becky hurtled herself forward, slamming into Spike head-on in midair. With a sickening crunch, the two of them came crashing down. The other Giants came thundering over now, landing on top of them, one after the other.

The ref blew his whistle. "Play dead!"

The entire stadium rose to their feet. Spike was so close to the goal line, no one could tell if he'd scored or not.

"He's over!" Kevin insisted from the Cowboy sideline.

"We stopped 'em!" Danny chanted from the Giants' bench.

The two coaches ran out onto the field and started pulling bodies from the pile.

"He scored!"

"No way. He was short!"

Danny helped Becky to her feet, revealing Spike still pinned beneath her. The ref blew his whistle. Spike was half a foot away from the goal line. "No touchdown," he shouted.

The Giants were almost weeping for joy. "No touchdown! No touchdown!" They were so thrilled they almost didn't hear the ref's whistle: "Giants' ball!"

● ● ● ● ●

Danny stood over his team, watching as Becky and the boys traded the highest high-fives of their whole lives. "Well, you did it," he told them, his voice trembling with emotion. "You stopped 'em. Now, who wants ice cream?"

His team stared up at him.

"But, Coach!" Hanon was the first to speak. "There's still four seconds left."

"Yeah. We can't quit now!" squeaked Jake Berman.

"We could try and win!" shouted Tad.

"Yeah!" the others cheered. "Let's win."

There was one more surprise as Junior Floyd stepped up to Danny. He was standing tall now, his helmet on his head. "Put me in, Coach," he implored. "I'm ready to play."

Danny struggled to keep his cool. "All right," he said evenly. "If that's the way you wanna play, go for it." He turned to Nubie. "You got a play for this situation?"

Nubie started punching buttons on his computer. He squinted as the portable printer started spewing out pages of data. "Yeah! This might just work . . . ." He handed a page to Danny. "The Ol' Fumblerooski," he said slyly.

Danny stared at the page as a slow smile spread across his face.

● ● ● ● ●

Junior was lined up over center at the four-yard line. Becky was at running back, behind him. Spike snarled at her across the line of scrimmage.

"You're mine, Pompom!"

"Hike!" The ball was snapped back, and the Cowboy defense saw Junior hand it off to Tad on the right. As the Cowboys surged forward, Tad leaped forward and left like a deer pursued by gun-crazy hunters. Murphy and Briggs took off after him, but before they could make a tackle, Tad handed off to Becky going right. As she sprinted downfield, the entire Cowboy team swept after her.

On the sideline, Kevin's face went red as he realized what the Giants were doing. "She doesn't have the ball!" He started shouting to his team, "Fumblerooski! Fumblerooski!" But the Cowboys were too involved with the play to listen.

Johnny threw a block for Becky, but he was no match for Spike's bulk. Spike brushed Johnny aside and put a solid hit on Becky. She went down hard. "Game over!" Spike yelled in triumph. "Spike rules!"

Becky rolled over and held up her hands. Spike's jaw dropped — she didn't have the ball! Becky grinned. "Spike stinks," she said. Spike looked around in total confusion. If Becky didn't have the ball, who did?

Then he saw where the ball was: in the hands of Rudy Zolteck.

When the ball had been snapped, Junior had carefully placed it behind Zolteck's left foot before faking the hand-off to Tad. The whole Cowboy team had been drawn away from the ball. Now Zolteck was lumbering downfield, with Hanon alongside as an escort. Not one Cowboy was within twenty yards, but Zolteck was running out of steam.

The Cowboys were up and running. Patterson was closing, with Murphy right behind. Zolteck knew he couldn't outrun them. At the last second before he felt hands grab his shirt, a glimpse to the side showed Junior there now, and in desperation, Zolteck heaved the ball back toward him. The ball bounced once, and landed perfectly in Junior's hands. That was the last thing Zolteck saw before he hit the dirt.

Junior zigzagged, dodging Briggs. He was only about twenty yards from the end zone, but there was a line of Cowboys between him and a score. He could only see one open teammate, Jake Berman. No one was more surprised when Junior threw a lateral to Jake than Jake himself.

Jake felt his arms close around the ball. He froze for a second, and then started a dash for the end zone. There was no one in front of him. His skinny legs pumped for all they were worth. "Go for the kill, Jakester!" snarled his mother from the stands. Jake smiled.

"I'm gonna score a touchdown!" he sang out as he ran. "I'm gonna score a touchdown!" His helmet bounced around on his head, but he didn't pay it any attention. As Spike watched in horror, Jake dashed across the ten-yard line, the five-yard line. No one was after him. Little Jake Berman was going to take it all the way into the end zone!

On the sideline, Danny clenched his hands together as if in prayer. "One time, baby! One time!"

Jake crossed the goal line.

"Tooooouchdown!" Clip Carson bellowed into the microphone.

Blinded by his helmet, Jake couldn't tell when to stop running. He kept on going until he smacked directly into the goalpost. But he didn't care. The Little Giants had won!

Pandemonium broke out in the stands. Cowboy parents were rubbing their eyes in disbelief. Giant parents and fans were rubbing their eyes in wonder. Little Timmy's father raced down to the sideline and blasted the cannon three times in a row.

• • • • •

As the town rushed out on to the field, Mr. Hammersmith flopped down on the Cowboy's bench and started bawling. "We lost!" he sobbed. Spike patted him on the shoulder. "Get a grip, Dad," he said. "It's gonna be okay . . . ."

And in the end zone, Patty Floyd threw her arms around Danny. "You were great, Coach!"

• • • • •

Danny blushed. "Thanks," he said. "Uh, Patty . . . I was wondering . . . . Would you be interested in having dinner with me?"

She leaned over and kissed him. Danny couldn't tell if that was a "yes" or a "no." "It's fine if you want to think about it."

Patty laughed. "Danny, the answer is yes, okay? But . . . " she paused, " . . . we might have to make it a double date." She pointed to the other side of the field where Becky and Junior were walking along together, holding hands.

Danny grinned at her. Then he looked up and saw a very depressed Kevin standing at the end of the field.

Danny turned to Patty. "Uh . . . I gotta go talk to someone." He started across the field to his brother.

Kevin saw him coming and jogged over. They met at the fifty-yard line.

"Well, it looks like you're the new coach around here," Kevin said. "Congratulations." He put out his hand and Danny shook it. Then Kevin handed him the game ball.

Danny smiled. "One town, one team, huh?" he said softly.

Kevin winced. "And if you're ticked off 'cause I've been so tough on you, too bad," he said stubbornly. "If I hadn't, you never would have beaten me today."

Danny nodded. "You're right," he said simply. "Anyhow, my kids were wondering if, uh . . . ."

"They could tar and feather me on Main Street?"

"No! They were wondering if your little thugs might want to play with the Little Giants."

Kevin was clearly surprised. "What are you saying?"

"I'm saying, we're forming one team — one team for the whole town. And they can be part of it, if they want."

Kevin was silent a moment. "Thanks, Danny," he said. "I'll tell the boys." He slowly turned away. "See ya"

"And Kev," Danny called after him. "Is there such a thing as having two head coaches on a team?" Danny smiled.

Kevin frowned, "No."

"What about if the head coach doesn't know as much about football as the other coach?" Danny gave Kevin a pleading look.

Kevin smiled. "Okay, Danny, you've got a deal. Oh, and . . . about that other thing . . . . You know, the little bet we made? You're not gonna hold me to that, right?"

Danny raised his eyebrows. "Hey, you think I'd throw my own brother out into the street?"

Kevin looked relieved.

"No, Kev," Danny went on, "there's always gonna be a job for you at my Chevy dealership. We'll start you on straight commission, see how it works out, and —"

"Danny! Please tell me you're joking," Kevin pleaded. "Come on, Danny. There must be something else you want."

Danny pretended to think. "Well, now that you mention it, there is one little thing. It's nothing, really. Just a little something I've been thinking about for a while." He glanced up at the water tower. Kevin glanced up at it, too.

"Remember when we were kids, Kev, and you said . . . ."

Kevin turned to him. "You can't be serious, Danny?"

"Oh, but I am, Kev. I am."

Kevin threw up his hands. "Okay, you win," he sighed good-naturedly. "After all, I guess I did kind of promise — back when we were kids and everything."

"Yup. You sure did."

Shading his eyes, Danny gazed up at the water tower again. He could almost see how it would look with "Welcome to Urbania. Home of Kevin and Danny O'Shea!" painted across it in big red letters. Suddenly, he started to grin.

It was going to look just great!